LLOYD JONES

Lloyd Jones is the author of several novels and short story collections including the critically acclaimed *Hand Me Down World* and *Mister Pip*, winner of the Commonwealth Writers' Prize Best Book Award and shortlisted for the Man Booker Prize in 2007. He lives in Wellington, New Zealand.

The Man in
the Shed

LLOYD JONES

JOHN MURRAY

First published in Australia by The Text Publishing Co. and in New Zealand by Penguin
New Zealand 2009

First published in Great Britain in 2011 by John Murray (Publishers)
An Hachette UK Company

1

'Who's That Dancing with my Mother?', 'Broken Machinery', 'Swimming to Australia', 'The
Simpsons in Russia', 'Where the Harleys Live', 'Lost Cities', 'The Waiting Room' first published
in *Swimming to Australia and Other Stories*, Victoria University Press, 1991.
'Amateur Nights' first published in *This House Has Three Walls*, Victoria University Press, 1997.
'Going to War for Mrs Austen' first published in *More 103*, January 1992.
'What We Normally Do on a Sunday' first published as 'Searching for Space', in *Sport 22*, ed.
Fergus Barrowman, Autumn 1999.
'The Thing that Distresses Me the Most' first published in *The Best New Zealand Fiction*, Vol. 3,
ed. Fiona Kidman, Random House, 2006.
'Dogs' first published in *The Best New Zealand Fiction*, Vol. 1, ed. Fiona Kidman, Random
House, 2004.
'Still Lives' first published in *Are Angels OK?* eds. Bill Manhire and Paul Callaghan, Victoria
University Press, 2006.

A CIP catalogue record for this title is available from the British Library

ISBN 978-1-84854-482-6
Ebook ISBN 978-1-84854-490-1

Typeset in 12.5/17 Granjon by Servis Filmsetting Ltd, Stockport, Cheshire

Printed and bound by Clays Ltd, St Ives plc

John Murray policy is to use papers that are natural, renewable and recyclable products and made
from wood grown in sustainable forests. The logging and manufacturing processes are expected
to conform to the environmental regulations of the country of origin.

John Murray (Publishers)
338 Euston Road
London NW1 3BH

www.johnmurray.co.uk

the man in the shed

There are times when he fights back in his own quiet way, when, suddenly and without any prompting that I can see or think of, he will lay down his knife and fork and look across the table at me as though I am a view or the answer to something, and then he will just get up and walk away from us as if none of this is right, this kitchen, even the faces around the table. The family has been misplaced or he has come home to the wrong house. And by the time Mum and I have made it to the kitchen window he is out in the drive looking in both directions. He is looking for something or someone that never arrives. In this way Dad seems to live on hope.

The man in the back shed is the problem. He used to eat all his meals with us. Now it is only when Dad is at work or out somewhere—the latter is a problem because he isn't ever just *out somewhere*. He is either leaving or returning, and so, even when he isn't with us at mealtime, the thought of him arriving at the door or even walking down the street is a concern shared around the kitchen table. We sit on our nerves. We look up and stop chewing at the littlest of things—a cough, the dog stirring in its basket, a raised voice from outside. We all have our own lists because not everyone looks up at the same particular moment.

The man from the shed lifts the soup bowl to his lips. This must be a European thing because both Pen and I have noticed it passes without criticism from Mum, which is odd because both of us recall a whack over the knuckles the first time we did the same. Now, watching the man from the shed reminds us of what a natural thing it is to do, and what a pain in the arse it is to have to scrape around with your spoon for the dregs. When he raises the bowl to his lips, his eyes float up to look at Mum. She is staring at her own soup and not saying anything. From the time she sat down she hasn't spoken. At her elbow is the empty space at the table where Dad usually sits.

She doesn't look up until we hear the latch on the

gate—and then we all do. The man from the shed puts his bowl down and gets up from the table. He looks at Mum. He looks thoughtful, as though he is considering something. He says, You're going to have to tell him. Mum nods at her soup. The back door opens. We can hear Dad pulling off his boots. We can hear the old dog rise from her half-bitten cane basket, beating her tail with happiness. The front door closes and at last Mum looks up. She smiles bravely—one each for me and Pen, and we are given to understand that we should forget what we just heard, that it is business as usual. We should, if we can, act like the dog. That would be nice.

But, in fact, when Dad comes into the kitchen both me and Pen jump up from the table. Her boyfriend Jimmy Mack is parked outside. He's been there the past half hour, waiting for her to finish her soup. I don't have such an excuse. I mutter, I'll be off to my room. That's where I am now, sitting on my bed. The waiting is going on and on. I had imagined the telling would happen as soon as me and Pen exited the kitchen. So I am surprised when I hear doors open-ing—the kitchen, then the front door, then the doors to the car. I have an idea Mum and Dad are on their way to the beach. That's where they usually take themselves when something needs to be said. Pen is out in Jimmy

Mack's car. The TV room is sitting in darkness, waiting for someone to turn up. I don't want to go in there. Nor do I want to go out to the backyard. So I'm stuck in my room.

I'm in bed when I hear the car pull up. Doors open and close—the car, then the front door to the house. There's no slamming. No raised voices. I listen out for something between them but not a word travels up the hall. I hear the light switches and then, some time after, by which time I am sitting up in bed in the dark, a stillness envelops the house. At a late hour I wake to someone walking up and down the hall.

In the days that follow I never once hear it said—not by either of them—that she is pregnant.

Months later it is still not talked about. There are indirect references. Some morning sickness, but in Mum's case just 'feeling a bit off'. Some backaches—and of course the indisputable fact of her stomach ballooning out, and her waddling walk and her difficulty in bending down to pick up anything from the floor. But none of this is ever commented on.

We are waiting—that is what we are doing. The waiting has weight; it has ballast. It loads up the house. It pushes back at the walls. It draws you to the windows. There are eight in our house and I've looked out every one of them. There are other times when the world suddenly jolts everyone forward. We come to, and remember that there are lives to be lived and we move back to reclaim those old parts of our selves. Dad has his work to escape to. Pen has Jimmy Mack. I have school and the beach. The beach is also a refuge for Mum and the man in the back shed.

The man in the shed does not enter the sea as the rest of us do, wading and willing ourselves deeper and deeper, braving the rings of agonising cold as they rise up our bodies. The man in the shed stands in the shallows, this tall lean man, washing his legs down, washing his arms down, splashing his face. The tide shuffles in and washes around his ankles. He stoops down and cups some water in his hands, and this he applies to his face and neck. Mum is already up to her waist. She is hurrying to get beyond the sandbars. At the same time she keeps looking back over her shoulder. The beach is more than a kilometre long but she is interested only in a small part of it.

I am sitting down at the rocky end of the beach, but I can see everything. When I tire of watching them I pull on my flippers and mask and swim out to the kelp beds, and there I lie on top of the sea, spying on fish as they come and go through the hanging curtain of kelp. The fish move without hurry. They seem to move for no other reason than they can. The first super-sized shopping centre has recently landed in our neighbourhood and I've noticed shoppers there moving up and down the aisles in the same dazzled state as these fish moving in and out of the kelp. They are looking for something. They're just not sure what it is.

A few days from now a violent storm will tear the kelp from the seabed and fling it up on the beach and we will move across it with our heads down like those salvage teams in white overalls sifting through the assemblage of a plane wreck. There will be a variety of pale limpid seaweed with a reddish stain and a ribbon-like fish that I have never seen on my snorkelling expeditions. A fish like that is a reminder of how close we are in our everyday lives to the unknowable. On another day we will stand in a circle around the treasure of a drag net—looking down at the albino eel, an elephant fish, and a tiny seahorse grinning impishly as if it had just flopped out of a gift shop. Then there are all the other things, which we cannot identify.

I couldn't place his accent when he first arrived—even the notion of arrival does not quite get at the surprise of him standing beneath the porch light. When I went to answer the door I wasn't expecting him. No one was. We had been eating and talking around the dinner table. I can't remember what was said, other than this sudden and unexpected smiling tolerance for one another, and then came the knock and we all looked up and Dad said to me, Why don't you go and see who it is?

My hair was still wet and gritty with sand. Earlier in the day a massive cruise ship with black sides had squeezed through the harbour entrance, and on the far side of the harbour we crashed ashore on the bow waves and each time we landed arse-up in a wash of foaming water and shingle, a tumble of limbs, joy dripping off our faces at our out-of-control lives.

There was his accent. The next thing I noticed about him under the porch light was his clothes. They clearly marked him out as a foreigner. His grey flannels turned up at the cuffs. A neat seam ran down the middle of the trouser leg—it wasn't overdone but you did notice it, that and the clean grey and the ease of the material itself. It wasn't just the clothes but the way he wore them, the way they sat on him. He wore his blazer off one shoulder. And his smile—unlike Jimmy Mack's, say, which came down to two tiny points of a smile set deep in the centre of his black eyes—his smile was evenly spread across his face. It generated warmth. Within a minute of his entering the kitchen we were all smiling, although who could have said at what or why?

I was already in bed when later that night I heard voices in the hall. I heard Mum say, Perhaps we can put him on the couch. *Perhaps* was one of my mother's favourite words. *Perhaps* belonged to the margins of the world we roamed in—it was an expression of possibility. In my mother's use the word had a generosity of spirit pushing from behind, a kind of moral consideration. Some time later I heard them set up the couch. In the morning I found him on it with his face turned away. Instead of a pillow, his hand rested under his cheek. I crept past and opened and closed the door with the same consideration. I did not want to wake him. The next time I saw him he was in the kitchen, at ease in his neatly turned-up flannels. His face was large, larger than either of my parents' faces.

A week later he was still in our lives. There must have been some sort of discussion. In any event I had missed it. There wasn't room in the house. So we parked him in the shed out the back. Mum made some curtains. Dad rustled up a camp stretcher. The neighbours flung a floor rug over the fence, which they kindly said they had no use for.

Another neighbour we didn't know well, except as some kind of scientist, turned up at the door with a chess set under his arm. As I was the one who answered, his interest went straight over my shoulder to probe the interior of our house. He said he'd heard we had a visitor. Might he be up for a game of chess? Right on cue our man emerged smiling out of the dark hallway in his white shirt and dark slacks. He'd just come out of the shower. His hair was wet. He came towards us buttoning his shirt at the wrists.

Dad was still at work. Pen was out somewhere with Jimmy Mack. So it was just me and Mum for an audience. Our man took the window seat for himself and gestured to one of the chairs for our neighbour. That end of the kitchen filled with an energy it didn't know well. It was a particular kind of silence that amplified the sounds of the outside world. A passing car's gear shift made our lives feel all the more stationary, and in the silence that filtered back down I could hear the dog scratching herself and the thrushes in the guttering. Outside the window the hedge top was shiny and twiggy. Overhead the roofs cracked in the heat. It was a day for the beach. But there we were, packed in around the chess set on the kitchen table. Our man smiled a lot which, on this occasion, I took to be a show of confidence. The smile was for the walls of the kitchen, for the moment at hand, but it was clear that Mum thought the smile was for her, and her face, I noticed, lit up.

Our neighbour drew himself over the board. He squinted down at the pieces, looked surprised, whistled through his stained teeth, then sat back in his chair, folded his arms contentedly, hugged himself, now very sure of himself. Then he dropped his arms at his side and sat upright. Checkmate, said our man.

Dad could ask me, as he did later on, how the day had gone and I would tell him it was all right. The neighbour from across the way came over for a game of chess with our man. And although what I said was true enough, it failed to pass on those things that were surely more interesting than pieces moving about a board. I could not begin to tell him about this new atmosphere that the kitchen hadn't known before. I could not draw his attention to an exchange of smiles that said so much more than I could say. Things had happened but under cross-examination I wouldn't have known how or what to say they were. A description of the thing itself would lead nowhere useful.

One afternoon we found ourselves alone in the back-yard. The man in the shed stood looking around and grinning at everything. I couldn't think what to say to him. Finally he said, Why don't you show me your neighbourhood?

I took him up the street. We passed the house with the woman and the cats. We passed the house with the long grass. A Maori family had moved in recently. We still didn't have much to do with them. There followed a stretch where the front lawns were mown and the flowers almost too bright to be real. We passed the house where in the winter I had seen an ambulance pull up. I'd waited until the stretcher came out bearing old Mrs Quinn who, I learnt later when Mum read out her obituary, had actually taught at my school and was a one-time high jump champion, but that was a long time ago. When I saw her she was covered in tarpaulin and strapped to the stretcher. I thought of asking the man from the shed if he had any explanation for the straps but instead I walked quickly on without saying anything about Mrs Quinn or the stretcher. It remained a private moment and a few minutes later I was pleased I hadn't said anything. Mrs Quinn was my first dead person.

We walked on as far as the green metal fence at the end of the road, and there we turned and walked all the way back up to where our street met with the main drag down to the beach, and where, on the corner, we stopped to smell the damp sea air. A flock of seagulls was winging it up the valley. Bad weather was on the way. At this time of the year it would be just a one-day wonder, what we called a clearing storm—it would be cold, all wind and fury, and then we would wake to a world perfectly still and new, and by the afternoon the roofs up and down the street would be cracking in the heat and all the dogs would be looking for shadows to crawl into.

Now we turned and walked back the way we'd come until we reached the shingle drive. Here the man in the shed stopped and looked back up the street. It was as though he thought there might be something else. But there wasn't anything else. This was it. You live in a nice neighbourhood, he said. I hadn't ever thought of it as a nice neighbourhood or, for that matter, a bad one. It was just where we lived. I wished I could have shown him something. An event of some kind. Briefly I entertained walking him back to Mrs Quinn's. Instead I shrugged.

Just a few years earlier the Sputnik had broken free of the earth's atmospheric crust. Anyone who has hit a tennis ball higher than a house roof will understand the ambition of the Sputnik crashing through all those layers of containment. The Sputnik provided pictures, which were published in our local newspaper. For the first time in human history it was possible to look back at the planet we inhabited.

More modestly, the edge of the sea served the same purpose. There, unable to venture further, we could stop and turn away from the horizon and look back at our lives. As the tide came in, bottom feeders slid across our fading footprints and our collapsed sand battle-ments. If you were to wait a few more hours for the tide to turn it was as if you'd never passed this way. You were strangely free of the historic fact of having walked in a particular direction and touched this piece of the earth. The wet sand sparkled, then it turned to slate under a passing cloud. Suddenly it was ready for the world to start over, to create new footprints. Down there *perhaps* was the way forward, towards temptation.

I watch Mum make a small pile of her clothes, watch the way she steps out of her leather sandals. She pulls a white swimming cap down over her ears. She suffers earache in cold water. Without her hair, her face looks older, more mannish. As she enters the sea the man from the shed does his washing-of-limbs thing. I watch Mum push on into deeper water. She isn't the fastest of swimmers—her stroke is a bit laboured and the man from the shed easily catches her. Once he does he lounges around in the sea; he lies in it, lies on his back looking up at the anchored cloud, then rolls over and with a few powerful strokes has caught up with her again.

When the forecasted rain arrives in a heavy squall I hurry to the bus shelter by the car park. When rain falls onto sand the sound is soft. The world is suddenly packed with cotton wool. It hears nothing and yet at the same time its capacity to hear feels infinite. The sand will absorb all. On the History Channel, whenever the troops stagger ashore under fire, the sand explosions are spectacular, sand rising with volcanic gusto but also falling back into place, to tidy up after itself—or others, as it were. Rain is almost pleasant when you swim in the sea. Rain smooths out the waves, creates tiny pools that exist only for the moment they are observed.

From the bus shelter I stick my head out into the weather to see Mum stumble into the trench inside the sandbar. The man from the shed offers a steadying hand. She accepts it. As they climb up the shelf she takes her hand back to place against her thigh. And I breathe out again, relieved she has taken her hand back. I am relieved because as far as I can see there isn't a story in what I am seeing. There isn't anything down there that I might report when Dad comes home and asks after my day. They are back on damp sand. I look further up the beach. A wind could blow and nothing would disturb that packed sand. Their footprints will be there the next day. The larger and slightly unaligned right footprint of the man from the shed and Mum's own trailing pitter-patter prints, patient, dependable. The rain had blown in halfway through their swim and left everything plastered down. Now it was pouring off house roofs, down copper and plastic guttering to run ankle-deep in pavement gutters, a grey tide of suburban murk moving towards the storm drains. In another twenty minutes or so a black tide will burst from the discharge pipes at either end of the beach and a black stain will push out to sea. I poke my head around the corner of the bus shelter for one more look. Mum and the man from the shed have gathered up their clothes. They are running for the changing sheds.

Later that night Dad pokes his head in my bedroom door to ask how my day went, and did I make it down to the beach. And without compromising myself or telling a lie, I say, It rained. Even though it is dark I can make out his relief. That's the story, he says.

What he already knows—I get the feeling he'd like more of that.

There are days, though, when the waiting turns Dad to stone. His eyes turn grey, and at such times I can almost detect the redundancy of the industrial age upon his skin and pouring out his nostrils. Down at the beach where Pen and I have taken off in different directions, he stands alone on a midden of broken glass, amid sun-cracked condoms and other Saturday-night cast-offs, which exercises his mind in regard to my sister. Pen is following the edge of the tide. She is walking into unpatrolled waters without a care in the world—which is bullshit, I know, because I am certain she is very alert to the interest she is creating. I can hear the doors opening and closing up at the car park. Mum doesn't appear to share Dad's concern. She goes on combing the shoreline for cats' eyes. She collects them for the drive. From out of her shadow my sister emerges with the same detachment, though she is not quite indifferent, because she is walking the way I have seen her do many times in town where she will turn her head to check her reflection in the passing shop-windows. One of the faces up at the sea wall is Jimmy Mack's. He has been banned from seeing my sister for one month. It was Dad's idea. I don't know why. He was the one who sat explaining to Jimmy in his car outside our house.

The seagulls make their racket. Somehow they save the day. They glide on the wind. They drop shellfish over the car park. They make you feel as though you have been on an outing. Now something big and care-free lands nearby: I kick it back to the playing kids and the beach ball floats unevenly seeking both buoyancy and a place to land. And I go back to grinding my heels into the sand. I want to see how deep they will go. I want to see how far they will go.

*

On another day, a burner—along this same stretch of fine sand, between umbrellas with their splatter of daisies and suns, the spread towels—sunbathers lie everywhere in a home brew of vinegar and oil. The quick death of melanoma goes unmentioned, along with Mum's pregnancy. The world we cannot see has heaped clues in a neat line along the high-tide mark. Piles of jellyfish with their blue stingers have kept a lot of people out of the water. But not Mum and the man from the shed. They are doing their laps between the moored rafts. Dad looks down at a woman's bra half filled with sand that washes back and forth in the tide and looks up again, concentrating on the estuary much farther down the beach.

I don't know where Pen is. But she is not here with us. It's just me and Dad today and we are walking with our fishing tackle to Sandy Point.

There is a smell of blood in the air. Where we intend to fish, the sea bears a red stain. The blood is from the meatworks. In the killing season—now—fish swim in from the depths to feed at the edge of the red mealy stain that began with stock moving along the pens, a stun gun knocking the sweet life out of their skulls, and the beast hooked up and flensed by men in white caps and white overalls and white gumboots who carve it up into the hindquarters and forequarters, all those juicy joints of the butcher's shopwindow. The blood is sluiced along pipes laid from the works to an outfall buried under the lid of the sea.

And here the fish come in their droves. Even today, in what would normally be un-fishlike conditions. Too much sun, too much light, too much daylight bombarding the surface of the sea. Yet there they are, cutting up the water, a frenzy of fish, some leaping from the water in sheer terror at the passing shadow of a kingfish. I have seen one chase a kahawai all the way onto the rocks, where a grateful fisherman picked it up with one gloved hand and with the other sliced open its gills, blood spurting out and a confused fear draining the fish's shocked eyes.

Earlier that morning I'd come into the kitchen to find Mum and Dad already up, a remnant of the night upon them both. Silence and anger looking for some-where to alight. Mum with one leg twisted around the other, all her attention focused on the bench top. She waited until Dad had finished his toast and gulped down the last of his tea. She waited until he had packed his lunch. She waited until after he pulled on his boots in the hall. Then, just as the door was about to close, she called out—in passing—that she planned to go swimming—ocean swimming, as she calls it—that afternoon. The door didn't close immediately. Neither of us could see what Dad made of that announcement. I pictured him on the porch, his head at a tilt, which is the way he usually looks after leaving the house and has stopped halfway across the lawn to wonder if he's remembered everything.

Mum stood slightly bent in the direction of the door. She was trying to judge the silence. There was no movement—no sound, nothing at all to go on. She called out—again, as if in passing. She said, It's been such a long time. I thought it would do me some good.

The front door closed quietly, so quietly I heard the snip. I moved to the window to see Dad walk up the garden path. He went out the gate without a second look. Mum was late arriving. She caught the back of his head just before it moved out of sight by the neighbour's hedge. She had missed what I had seen, and not just this time either: my father's tremendous ability to absorb pain.

He came home early from work that afternoon and we drove to the beach. He brought along his fishing gear as if to show that his interest lay elsewhere, and not with Mum swimming stroke for stroke with the man from the shed, but along the estuary where the fish were cutting up the sea.

Where I happen to walk belongs to neither one of those two worlds. My sandbar is its own complete kingdom. Right then I could not think of a better place to be. Deep water lay either side of me. It was just a matter of sticking to this splinter of sand. To people sitting in their overheated cars above the beach I'm sure the tidal transition appears slow and benign. But if you happen to stand at the edge of a sandbar you can see the crumbling sand and the darting shadows of fish following the current to deeper water. That is something we can all understand: the fear of being left behind.

Dad does not look back. He labours on in the heavy grey sand, trailing smoke. I step lightly, knowing as I do that my landbridge is temporary, and even though it gives an impression of substance and reliability it is, in fact, in the process of turning into beach or sinking into the tide. I can feel the fragility of the arrangement through the soles of my feet. The world and my place in it suddenly and surprisingly feel provisional. I had always had the idea that the world was a place specially created for me. And that the task of my parents—in fact their whole reason for being—was to point things out and to get me started.

Now I can see the sandbar is going to deliver me back to the main beach and Dad's own footprints. When I get there I try stepping in them, then give up. I'm not all that keen anyway as his left footprint is set at an odd angle from carrying the fishing gear on that side of his body and I don't feel like turning my leg inside out to match him, to pretend to be weighed down by what he is.

His legs are so pale, without any sea grace—more suited, I think, to the garden and welding, activities demanding prodigal patience. He likes fishing, though, and there is no place like the estuary when the fish are running.

I stop once more to see where Mum and the man in the shed are. Beyond the rafts a bank of cloud turns everything the colour of bronze. I wait for the world to re-emerge. And out it comes again—blue and dazzling. Boats with white sails swan about. The sea breeze has dropped away. I feel on the brink of something—where I'm not quite cold but nor am I burning for a swim either. It's a summer's day but so far not one to remember.

When we get to the estuary all the best places are taken. Everywhere are plastic buckets with fish tails hanging out, chopping boards and kitchen towels smeared with blood and fish scale. We pass one fisherman after another, some sitting in the sand looking up at the tips of their surfcasters. They are men trying to divine the presence of fish from the hopeless position of a landlocked life. For the first time in what feels like

weeks Dad is moving with urgency. He stumbles on, slip-sliding in the sand, me in tow. All around us the braking mechanisms on reels are shrieking and the grey water is chopped and cut by fishing lines pulled taut, rods bending and unbending in the rod-holders. Surfcasters are pulled back in a great dragging arc, as if the fishermen are attempting to pull the seabed up with two hands. Fish scales are stuck to gumboots—the standard white issue from the meatworks—whittled off fish which already look like the supermarket variety, their guts scooped out and thrown back into the estuary from which they just emerged intact a minute earlier, and now the gulls are flying down to carry off the dangling guts in their beaks.

There is this awful feeling that while we have not entirely missed the show we are late to it. One fish leaps in the air and for a split second its round eye makes contact in the same way as a face in a passing bus window. The fishing gear is banging against Dad's side as we struggle for footing in the subsiding sandbanks. He doesn't even notice when a cigarette butt falls from his mouth. He dumps the bag and starts connecting the sections of the surfcaster, threads the line through the hoops, ties on the lure with its tiny red plastic tongue fluttering lightly against the barbed hook. The tips of his fingers are callused with thick layers of skin the colour of steel, which he cannot scrub off no matter how hard he tries and how often Mum used to badger him. But with those same hands I have seen him pick up gorse and not feel a thing.

He draws back the rod and when he casts there is that terrible and exhilarating shriek of reel. Something brightly reflective catches my eye. Spools of fishing line gather and gather around his feet as the shriek of the reel fades and is answered by the gulls. Blood is streaming down his cheek. The red lure is stuck there—he's hooked himself. It comes back to me, the way he carried through with the cast regardless, with complete faith, as if he was unaware of what he'd done. Now a look of rage overtakes him, a door-slamming rage. And he reaches up and tears the hook from his cheek. Tears it out as I've seen him tear the hook from the mouth of a kahawai. The first time I saw him do that he looked back at my shocked face and assured me, Fish don't feel a thing. They're cold-blooded buggers, he said. But as he rips that hook out of his own flesh he swears like a trooper— at the bastard of a thing, at himself, at the world for getting him tangled up like this. Blood streams down his face, drips onto his shirt collar. His face is red with shame. Slowly he winds in the slack line, his grey eyes locking me out because I am to blame as well.

*

At an age when he must have known I would be impressed he used to say he made fire engines, but what he really does is solder sheets of metal into a perfectly curved cylinder capable of holding upwards of twenty thousand gallons of water, enough, he tells me, to put out any mid-sized house fire. Now he brought his gear home at the weekend. His welding torch, his helmet and emulsifying fluxes. I helped him haul a number of steel slats and poles down the side of the house to the backyard. A plan to build a swinging garden seat was announced. But I also understood the unspoken part of the plan. He was out to place himself between Mum and the man in the shed. They would have to get past him while he knelt on the lawn in a shower of sparks.

It only took him a couple of weekends to build. Late one Sunday afternoon he stood up and pulled back his welder's helmet. His face was covered with sweat and hope. He said, Go inside and get your mother. When we came out he was rubbing the slats with a rag. Mum sat down on the swing and waited for the magic to arrive. She couldn't move it on her own. She tried and shook her head. She smiled down at the burnt grass between her dangling feet and said it wouldn't work. Dad was already heading for the workshop at the back of the garage. He'd identified the problem. Something to do with the structure needing more oil. With time, he said, it would improve. It was simply a matter of heavy parts knowing they could move.

Meanwhile the promise of ceremony had drawn out the man from the shed. Mum looked up and smiled as he crossed the lawn. He stood behind her and shoved with a gentle but firm hand and slowly the swing, smelling of newness and oil, slowly it began to move. The back of the swing rolled elegantly away from Mum's spine and she was smiling up at the man who'd made it work.

The few times I saw her in the swing after that, she sat without swinging, without wanting to, or caring to, it seemed. She held the link chain as her head turned to the shed at the end of the backyard. I wasn't sure if he was in there and, if he was, why he wouldn't come out. These days he was shy as a guinea pig.

The swing gave Dad the excuse he was after, but he sat in it without any evident sense of pleasure. He looked like a man sitting at a bus stop. He rolled a cigarette, smoked it, he took it out of his mouth; he studied the end of it, put it back in his mouth, took it out again and flung the butt over his shoulder. He looked at the time on his wrist. He sat there with folded arms until at last he pushed himself up and stood gazing at the sky. He had seen something noteworthy. Now he sat down again, with only the dog there to show interest. She lifted her snout then lowered it back to her front legs.

Another time I was looking on from the bedroom window when I saw him quickly stand up from the swing. He moved with such resolve that I felt both exhilarated and worried. He'd moved beyond view. I left the window and hurried down the hall to the back door. By which time he was retying an area of the sweet pea vine that had come away from the climbing structure.

I was too young to see their lives in full. These were the clues, gestures towards something that I couldn't properly comprehend. Mostly, though, it was anger, and inside the house it was as toxically present as fly spray. In the open door I saw their twin beds divided by a vanity. The room was as cold as any motel room I have slept in since.

By now I had stopped thinking of things for us to do together. Mostly I tried to avoid Dad. I could not bear to look at him directly in case he saw the pity I felt for him. So I crept around the house and calculated my movements on going where I knew he wouldn't be. I wasn't equipped to help him. I didn't have the words that he might need to hear. For all of that, I watched and I listened and I was curious to know more and to find out what I could without being direct about it.

From my bedroom window I could see the battered old tennis racquet and dog-bitten ball lying in the dry grass. Once the sight of those two things lying in easy proximity would have drawn me out there right away. But I kept away from the backyard. It was just in case. I didn't want to be seen talking to the man in the shed. The shameful fact is I didn't mind talking to him. I liked answering his gently plied questions because that was the shape of our conversation. He had to dig to get words out of me. And at this apparent resistance of mine he'd give me a little side-eyed look. These days his smile didn't extend beyond his eyes. It was a matter of loyalty to Dad that I made the conversation operate in this way. But one thing for sure: I didn't want to be talking to the man in the shed and to turn around and see Dad's face at the back window. I didn't know how to put out his sadness. Sure as hell I didn't want to add to it. So it meant avoiding the backyard and that's how I became estranged from those things which once had been such a big part of me—the racquet and the tennis ball, the shed too, which had once housed a pet sheep. These things were turning into memories. For the first time I was seeing how time sorted the world into current and past. Time touched everything. One afternoon when I stood at the back window, I realised with a sad sort of shock that nonetheless carried its own quick exhilaration that I had grown apart from the backyard. The disused swing and the man in the shed no doubt played their part. But, also, the backyard had come to represent something else. I didn't want to go out there because it would mean walking back into the old me who didn't know anything. When, in fact, I'd just decided I wanted to know the *next* thing. I preferred that to playing around like the dog snapping at fleas popping out of its own fur. I wanted to *know*.

One night I am woken by shouting in the TV room. Unusually it is Dad's voice, now Mum's hand-wringing whine and groan, now both, and I am expecting to hear the man from the shed, but instead what I hear is Pen sobbing, followed by feet marching down the hall. The front door slams with such violence my night-light briefly goes out before flickering back on.

The wounded air of the night lasted until breakfast, where I found Pen sitting at the kitchen table with Jimmy Mack. Jimmy smiled at me. A quick disapproving look from my sister removed the smile. And Jimmy settled for nodding down at the table. Pen's hair was wet. She looked as though she had been made to stand in a cold shower for twelve hours. She glanced up at me in the doorway then back at her bitten nails. She bit off some more. She flicked it off her fingertips and glanced up again. Seeing I was still there (I wasn't going to leave without my breakfast), she said through her fingers, I'm pregnant. Jimmy's face lit up again. He beamed at me across the kitchen and then seemed to remember the moratorium placed on all smiles and happiness and quickly fitted on his earnest school-leaver's face, of a year back, which I suppose was the best he could come up with to go with the stunning fact that he was going to be a father.

Again things happened without warning. I came home from school one day to find my sister's room bare. The bed was made, the sheets and blanket perfectly spread in a way that particular bed had never known. The carefully folded back part seemed to define the terminal sense of the room.

There was hardly anything that Pen didn't take with her to the motor camp.

Now we would stop by there on our way to the beach. My sister would be sitting barefoot on the steps of the caravan smiling wanly back at the world. We'd get out of the car, doors flying open, bounding cheerfulness in all directions. We were putting on a brave face. It was a hot and tiny caravan I stepped inside. It was shocking to see how my sister's world had shrunk to a small porthole view of the other caravans standing in a line, the long grass bursting up around the wheelhouse of each. It was clear. My sister's life had been put on hold.

I was glad to get back in the car and on our way. I was relieved to be driving away from the uncomfortable fact of her stalled life. The sky grew larger in the side windows of the car. From under the wheels came the popping sound of shells. A row of seagulls traced a line of roofs. The houses appeared to sway towards and away from the sea. The soft decay of the beach spread inland. Soon the windblown gardens petered out to sand and burnt lawn. The windows were thick with sea breath. The immensity of the sky mocked the idea of the houses. Why so much concrete in the drive? Why bother with the flower vase halfway along the window ledge? Yet on the way home it was possible to see these same houses quite differently. No longer were these weatherboards the tail end of our neighbourhood of well-maintained brick, but a continuation of the spin drift of the beach; they were another shelf on the shoreline.

We pulled in to the car park. Where we liked to walk was now covered in gloating tide. We got out anyway. That part was never in doubt. But it wasn't the same, restricted as we were to a narrow strip much higher up the beach, an area we usually passed up, and so close to the parked cars we could hear the tinny sound of their radios and the creak of heavy doors. Up here was a stew of beer cans, cigarette butts and weeds. Dad bent down to pocket a coin. He'd notice something like that but not the sand. Mum had fallen silent. Perhaps it was the thought of my sister in the caravan with Jimmy Mack. Jimmy had recently started his builder's apprenticeship. Jimmy's old man was a successful builder. It seemed the thing to do. Jimmy was going to build them a house one day.

I imagine these things preoccupied Mum as well as her own pregnancy and the man in the back shed. I would say the same went for Dad. There were days when he looked like he was single-handedly labouring under the effort to carry the entire world. His gaze slipped right off the face of the sea. If I looked closely I could see that his grey eyes weren't gazing at anything. That he was taking instruction deep from within and I had an idea he was wondering what to do about the man in the shed. The obvious thing was to show him the door. To kick him out on his pants. If it came to fisticuffs I was in no doubt who would win. Not that I seriously thought it would come to that but whenever I tried to think of something for Dad to do, of some means to take some pleasure, it always came down to a physical option. It was just as obvious that Mum was responsible for him staying on.

I have an idea—and again it is never said aloud—that the man in the shed will stay until his baby is born. And then what? Who could say? No one ever did.

On my sandbar I am able to think about these things more dispassionately. I have found a landscape that corresponds with something deep inside of myself but which I still don't fully understand. I can think about my parents without ever thinking their problems involve myself. Mum's behaviour, for example. I can come home to find her almost coltish, her eyes shining like a drunk's as she turns from the kitchen sink to find it is just me coming through the back door. Other times she is withdrawn and moody. And I'll come home to find her lying on the couch in the TV room, the TV off, her eyes tilted up at the clouds in the windows.

It is as though our lives are all in a state of drift. This is what waiting meant. You waited. That's what the man in the shed was sentenced to as well. Hours and hours of this idleness. Waiting for something to happen. Watched only by the dog, whose kennel Dad has shifted into the backyard. That's her snout lying in the grass; her watchful eyes are the only things that move.

In March the sea is two degrees warmer than at any other time of the year. By then the weather has settled into a predictable range. People are able to make plans. Mum went to the beach every day to pursue her ocean swimming. She'd found a place to put my sister's pregnancy, and possibly Dad and myself. She wasn't as overwhelmed as she had been just a few weeks earlier because she'd found she could just swim away from all of that. The man from the shed always went with her. They are always back by the time Dad gets home. On the clothes line, I've noticed, only Mum's togs are ever pegged up.

This particular afternoon is one out of the box. Blue skies with a late incandescent blaze that has everyone driving to the beach. When I get home Mum's togs aren't on the line and neither is she in the house. I have an idea she is in the shed. For ten minutes I stare out the window until the dog comes out of her kennel, walks in a small tired circle then returns to the dark of the kennel.

A few minutes later Dad shows up at the side of the house. I see him looking at the clothes line. Next thing he is inside the house shouting for me to pack the fishing gear.

By the time we get there the car park is full and we have to park back along the sea wall. At the edge of the tide a crowd of swimmers stand like sun-dazed cattle. Near the sand spit seagulls wheel and dive at the sea.

Dad is busy getting the fishing gear out of the boot, so he doesn't see Mum sink into the tide like someone crouching behind the bushes. She pushes off, head down, her quiet feet behind her. I wonder then if she's seen us. And, if she has, this new feeling I have is an unpleasant one. Stroking into her wake is the man from the shed. Those are his long legs and black togs. I have an idea they've spent the whole day down here. Dad locks the car. His blue work shirt, I notice, is patched with sweat. We climb the wall and drop down onto the sand and hotfoot it to the water's edge. Towards the point the fishermen are lined up on the sea side of the estuary. Some are familiar faces; some of them are known to Dad. I wonder if they know his story, his quiet anguish. I wonder because whenever we come near their eyes head out to sea.

I drop behind a step in order to sneak another look back at the swimmers. They have just left the first raft. I know Mum by her slow and methodical style. The sea parts and continues to part. Into this smooth water swims the man from the shed. Nothing about their swimming suggests gambolling joy. It is steadfast and mindful of form—to my mind a lower register of contentment. You could get the same from painting a fence.

An old Chinese guy with a steel rod calmly reels in

two fish at a time. There must be a dozen fish squirming and bending around his feet. He hasn't taken the time to stick and bleed them. There are still more to be caught.

Every third stroke Mum lays her head on one side to breathe. On the beach side she might have seen the fishermen wading out to the fish, and, beyond them, the sunlit windscreens. What she can't see is the direction taken by the spooked fish. Already the water is cutting up near her and the man from the shed. The faces of the fishermen, including Dad's, are tight with fear of the fish moving beyond the reach of their casts. I stand by Dad trying not to look at the purpling colour of his face or take personally his frosted eyes. So, he's seen her—that much is clear. In fact he looks to be on the brink of reaching down to pick up a rock to throw at her. He could always say he threw it to warn her of the kingies heading in her direction. The kingies are the fish causing the panic.

A whole line of us follows the disturbed water towards the rafts. Men with surfcasters, some of them twelve feet long, some with lures beaten out of dessert and soup spoons to look like the flashing scales of a fish. We advance into the tide, a line of us, up to where it laps at our crotches and we cast our home-styled lures to land in the frothing water.

All at once, rods bend and reels screech. By the dozen we are reeling in fat kahawai, big muscled fish that we walk backwards with and heave up onto the wet sand. Some of the fishermen quickly dig a hole in the sand and throw their catch into a soapy basin of water.

I happen to be inspecting a kingie someone has been lucky to hook when I look up to see everyone's eyes on a fisherman standing next to Dad. He is leaning back to get a sense of the weight of the catch. Some of the other fishermen have switched their attention to what he has on the end of his line. Everyone is waiting for the fish to break the surface so we can get a look at him. We follow the taut line dripping with light and we make searching glances to see where the sea might rip next. A large fish will usually show itself. But this fish is not behaving in the expected way. It does not come and go and there is no slack line to reel in. The same weight on the line is maintained, and the reel methodically clicks over. The fisherman tries switching the rod from his right to left hand, and now, to my surprise, he hands his rod to Dad. Dad hands his rod over in exchange. As they do so the stranger imparts some information on the breaking strain of his line. Now Dad wades into deeper water; he's up to his waist and that's when I see, along with the rest of the beach, that he is slowly reeling in Mum.

She is making some effort to help. It is clearly difficult for her. I have an idea she is hooked in the region of her back, which would account for her awkward crabbing movement. As Dad reels he walks towards her—reeling and walking, up to his chest now, and for her part Mum appears to be doing her best to work with Dad, coming to the pain as they did from different directions. I notice the disturbed water moving away. Some fishermen set off after it, but a number have stayed back to watch Dad and, I suppose, to see what will happen next.

It being mid-tide he's able to wade nearly halfway out to the raft, where he shifts the rod to his left hand and reaches his more powerful welder's arm around the front of Mum and scoops her out of the sea. He gets her into the shallows and that's where he hands the rod back to the fisherman. Taking great care he sits Mum down on the sand. She looks up but does not appear to see me. She's crying out to Dad to do something. To, please, please, get the thing out of her. Her shoulders are raised and her buttocks pushed out. I can see what she is trying to do. Fish do the same. They bend and arch as the hook is removed. Mum is trying to loosen the skin around the hook. I wonder if anyone else has noticed her stomach. It's large and resistant to the moment. It's as though it shouldn't be here, has separate business of its own to attend to. Dad glances up, sees me and waves me closer. He gets me to kneel down beside Mum. He gives me the instructions. I am to open her mouth and stick my forearm in.

He was so calm and matter of fact that I followed the instruction. He said it would probably hurt but not as much as it will your mum, remember that. And I did. He grabbed the skin around the hook and bunched it up. It gave him something to work with and had the effect of isolating the hooked-flesh part of Mum from the rest of her. When the moment came Mum made a muffled sound like that of someone trying to breathe through a pillow—then she spat my forearm out and swore loudly, a word I didn't know she had in her. That alone brought a smile to Dad's face. With a fat grin he held up the lure and a number crowded around for a closer look; one or two clapped. The man whose rod had hooked Mum patted Dad on the shoulder. Just beneath Mum's right shoulder you could see where the hook had embedded. A watery trickle of blood oozed down her back. I was inspecting the tooth marks over my forearm—Jesus, I was thinking, she's actually broken the skin. I was dying to show someone my own injury. I was looking up for a sympathetic face when I remembered the man from the shed. I found him treading water halfway between the raft and the beach.

How far away he seemed right then at that moment—almost, I felt, as if having taken this pause to see what was happening at the beach he might now drop his head back in the water and swim away out of our lives.

We drove home together. Mum, Dad and me. No one mentioned Mum's car. Hours later it was parked in the drive.

The next morning I came into the kitchen to find Mum at the table drinking tea and watching Dad eat his breakfast. I almost got away but she heard me. She closed a hand over the opening of her dressing-gown and swung around in her chair. She wanted to show me something. She pulled her dressing-gown off her shoulder to show her wound beneath the right shoulder blade. Then she asked to see my arm. She inspected the tooth marks then handed back my arm and thanked me. She said how brave I'd been to put up with that and not say a word. I didn't hear a whimper, she said. She asked Dad if he'd heard anything and he shook his head down at his plate of eggs. Nope, not a thing, he said.

Six weeks later beneath a screaming blue sky I trail after Dad along the coastal hilltops with the wind tearing at our faces and our eyes streaming. The same wind hares through the long grass. Pathways open up wherever the eye pitches next. Seagulls are blown sideways over the fence and farm gate, down beneath the gorse into ravines of shadow. Only a hawk holds its course.

We are looking for a place to bury a baby. I caught a glimpse of him after Dad pulled him off Mum and after he wiped the blood away. The baby is at home lying in a bed of cotton wool. A tiny wee thing—a boy, I noticed—curled up with spina bifida. Poor little bugger. That's his name at this point. Years later I will discover a different name on the death certificate. For now though he is poor little bugger. Dad is looking for a place to bury him and I've come along to help. Without saying as much we know the perfect place. It'll be where no one will notice a shovel scar left on the tops.

With the premature birth and death of poor little bugger I thought the man in the shed would leave our lives. But he didn't, and he showed no sign of going, and things began to slip back to how they were before.

Dad decided I would go and stay with Pen while he sorted out the 'mess' at home. School had started but that didn't seem to make any difference. His mind was made up. He drove me to the motor camp, as far as the white traffic bar at the entrance, and I was bundled out.

He gave me some money to give to my sister, plus a cake on a plate covered with a tea towel that Mum said she wanted back. A face came to the window of the office. When he saw who it was he waved me through. Along with the cake I carried my school bag with my toothbrush, underwear, a change of clothes and a sleeping bag.

There was a brilliant sky. The air smelt of dry heat and dog shit. Just about everything about the camp felt wrong. It was too good a day to be in a place such as this. I wished I was at the beach. The fine smell was from the soap factory across the golf course that backed on to the motor camp. I arrived at the caravan section. Most of them were shut up and their windows looked stale. The door to my sister's caravan was open. The radio was playing a Bee Gees song. My sister sat on the step with her nose in a magazine. She was unhealthily pale. Her legs were pink and white and under-exercised. Once upon a time she'd have been at the beach turning heads. But she no longer seemed to be of that world. She'd come out of another formed by plastic laminations and stainless-steel sinks and stale air. I poked my head inside. There was the table and the narrow beds where I guessed she and Jimmy slept. I was wondering where I was supposed to sleep when she pointed to the next caravan along, the one I'd stared at on previous occasions wondering who in this world of a sane mind would choose to live there.

You're in there, she said.

The door stuck when I tried to open it. My sister rolled her eyes and got up from the step. She wrenched it open. There was a dead fly on the laminated table. It wasn't squashed. It had died of boredom. I dumped my bag and we walked over to the showers and toilet block, then on to the kitchen. There we encountered another camper. A cheerful woman about Mum's age who after Pen introduced me said, So you're the proud uncle.

No one at home had pointed this out to me—this new status I'd acquired on the back of my sister's efforts. There was a trampoline near the office. We looked at it, and that was that. We went back to our caravans. My sister sat down in the door and reached for her magazine. After a few minutes she looked up, annoyed to see me there. You can't just stand there doing nothing. Do something. She reached around behind her for a magazine and gave it to me to read. I took it to my caravan step and for a while read about women dieting with spectacular results—down from 350 pounds to 130 pounds in twenty-one days. The weather girl on TV was getting married. Its pages were filled with stories of broken marriages, gossip, horoscopes, all of which gripped my sister. She read avidly and in a way I never saw her read at any other time.

I gave up and went off to explore. I followed a tall wire fence around the camp. I came upon some tents and three motorhomes. I found a creek and followed its bank. Mostly though I wondered what was going on at home. I stood at the fence separating the camp from another world where men strolled about with their golf clubs. I watched three men carrying two bags of clubs between them. They pushed one another and rolled away from friendly punches and howled with laughter at the insults flying between them. An aeroplane rose into the deep-blue yonder. A black bird swooped up and over the hurricane-wire fence. I moved along it to follow the shadows of the golfers falling across the mown grass until all I could hear was their laughter.

Later I blamed the golfers when my sister stood angrily before me demanding to know how I hadn't heard her calling for me. She needed milk but now I'd shown I couldn't be trusted and so she'd have to wait until Jimmy Mack finished work. I listened to her in silence (I'd been told not to upset her given her condition) and when she finished and dropped her head back inside a magazine I sloped back to the hurricane fence with the view of the golf course. The clouds stopped as soon as I looked at them and the blue sky shot away from my eyes. A plane gently rolled over and its wing dissolved in a flash of light. I thought of the large fish I'd seen at the start of the summer. Its plump white belly. Then it had moved back into the normal shadow of a fish. And I was left hyperventilating with excitement. There was just the irregular and non-comprehending stones on the seabed to look at but my heart was still beating wildly long after the event. In the days ahead the laughter and good-natured shouts and insults of the golfers reached deep inside the camp, and each time my sister looked up from her magazines she'd ask, Now what are you smiling at?

The grass hadn't been cut and, after a summer that had been long and hot, I felt straw scratching and poking my jandalled feet. One stalk actually broke the skin. I could feel it. I was even aware of blood. But I did nothing about it. I didn't stop to inspect it as I might once have but walked on with the stabbing pain and ooze of blood between my foot and the jandal. I walked on with a kind of dull fascination and insight. It was the first intimation that I wasn't my own invention at all. Already, at a certain level, I was turning into my father. A bit of a scratch, and blood was nothing. Because I had come into pain of a different kind, a vague under-the-skin disappointment that would not go away, that by comparison made a bit of blood nothing more than a mild curiosity.

All the time I wondered what was happening at home, day and night. I spent far too many hours standing at that hurricane-wire fence staring up at a slow-moving sky. I knew it was all about waiting. And I was really just waiting for the 'mess' at home to be over.

Towards the end of the month Dad came and got me. He told Pen that she and Jimmy were coming home. It wouldn't be that day but in a short while.

In the car Dad seemed changed—lighter. But I didn't look too closely because I had an idea he was looking out for exactly that. So we talked about sport. Rugby, actually. The pre-season weigh-in was coming up. This coming Saturday he wanted me to go over to the club and jump on the scales. He had an idea I would be going up to another weight division. It sounded like a good idea.

As we pulled in the drive the house drew up out of memory, its red brick reasserting itself after my time away. I went straight to my bedroom and before I'd dumped my things I stood at the window looking into the backyard, and I knew. I knew, without anyone telling me, the man in the shed had gone. That evening over dinner and later, before the TV, and for several days after, I waited and I waited, but nothing was ever said about his departure. For that matter, as I was surprised to discover, I couldn't even remember his name.

For a period the house reverberated with new energy. It was just the washing machine, the tumble and motion of wash, but there was something like the promise of newness, and a festiveness about the colours of the clothing spinning around in a porthole of glass that was infinitely more interesting and dynamic than the view from Pen's caravan window. The clothing came out of the wringer mangled and twisted and as stiff as cardboard—like bits of ruin, the holes and body spaces pressed out of existence.

I helped Mum peg up these scraps and I watched them become whole again. Sleeves filled with air, trouser legs bloated out, socks became whole again. A fresh wind restored purpose to these bits of clothing. One of the cast-offs was a shirt of Dad's that he couldn't fit into anymore but which I had grown into, an old denim shirt whose colour had faded. It was the fade I liked, the idea that the world had left its mark and now I had that bit of experience draped over me. That shirt gave me fresh measure against a world I was growing into.

Mum sat on the swing, watching me preen in Dad's shirt. Look at you, she said. She smiled and just for a moment I saw a glimmer of my sister. It was as though two selves momentarily met and passed through one another. I kept staring to see if I could hold on to the moment but it was gone. Mum's smile widened to a laugh. What are you looking at? she asked. What are you looking at?

the thing that distresses me the most

Let me start by saying this: my husband is not a bad man. I don't know the others all that well—Don Seeward, another from Auckland, Phil someone, James More from down south; 'Macca', I think they call him. Two others as well. Jim? I don't know. It doesn't matter. I've met Don once. The others I must have spoken to when they've rung the house for Stuart. They all work for themselves. Stuart knew Macca at university. The rest of them he's picked up over the years in different jobs.

Once a year they get together to discuss 'engineering issues'. This year it was Stuart's turn to host the occasion.

They flew in a few weeks before Christmas. It was a Saturday, a gorgeous day. On the way to taking the kids to the beach I stopped by Stuart's office to drop off a quiche and a cake. I could see them in the window gathered around the table in serious discussion.

'Knock, knock,' I said as I came in. They all leapt up like a bunch of thieves. Soon as they saw the food they gushed with compliments. Don gave me a hug and a kiss. Stuart introduced those faces I'd spoken to on the phone. They were happy about the food, and I was happy to leave them to it. I had the kids waiting outside in the car.

I saw them again, about five that afternoon. I drove by with the kids to find out Stuart's plans for dinner. I slowed down, and from the street I could see them in the window. They were standing now, beer bottles in hand. Someone must have been telling a joke because I could see Stuart in a convulsive fit with a hand over his mouth and Don, more expansive, as he leant back, mouth open wide. I thought Stuart could ring home later and let me know his plans.

I was glad to get home. Clara and Bella were acting up in the car. Both of them had got too much sun. At home I ran a bath for them. I made that old-fashioned emulsion my grandmother used to drum up from vinegar and rubbed it into their sunburn while they squealed and shouted. They were hungry, and around six Bella started whining for pizza. I said, 'Let's wait and see what your father's plans are.' It would be like Stuart to invite everyone back here; that would mean a quick run down to the supermarket. The pizza place is on the same block. I didn't want to make two trips. To take their minds off their stomachs I switched the telly on. I thought I would ring Stuart's office. But each time I picked up the receiver to dial I put it down again. If they were having fun I didn't want to be that grumpy bitch who brings things to a close. So I thought I would text Stuart. But the moment I had the idea I saw he'd left his mobile on the table. It was sitting with some papers I think he had meant to take to the office.

At seven o'clock I went to get pizzas. The girls came along for the ride in their pyjamas. There were half a dozen people in the shop so we had a bit of a wait. After giving the pizza order I thought I'd run by Stuart's office and gauge the mood. This time as I slowed down the blank window stared back. If anything the letters in the window were more bold—S. Richards. Engineer and Quantity Surveyor. Bella asked why we were back at Daddy's office. 'No reason,' I said.

I thought they must have gone off for a drink somewhere. A phone call to that effect would have been nice. But then perhaps Stuart was planning to come home soon anyway.

At home I put the pizzas out on the table and left the girls to it. I walked over to the phone and picked up the receiver. Bella looked up, a wedge of pizza jammed into her mouth. I put the receiver down and poured myself a glass of wine.

The girls watched the Saturday-night movie on Two. I tucked them into bed at ten and without complaint from either. This was as late as they had ever been up. They seemed to know that something about the night was different but they didn't want to know what it was. While they were watching TV neither one could shift their eyes from the screen.

There was some washing to bring in, and outside under the clothes line I looked up at the night. We live in one of the inner-city suburbs. There must have been some cloud about because the sky over the city was a sickly yellow. I heard a siren, and closer, maybe two streets over, the God-awful noise of a boy racer tearing up the night, and more distantly the steady rumble of the city. The washing still contained the airy warmth of the sun from earlier in the day, and for some time I stood there, with Stuart's shirts bunched in my arms, just listening.

I thought I would wait until midnight before taking

further action. I sat on the couch watching the minutes tick by. At the stroke of midnight I picked up the phone and rang the police. I was surprised to hear a woman's voice answer. It made me hesitate—just a bit. 'I don't know where my husband is,' I said. There was a pause at the other end, and in the intervening silence I heard the silliness of my complaint. Stuart wasn't missing. I was sure he knew where he was. I apologised and hung up.

There was nothing else to do but go to bed. I pretended to read. I managed to stay awake until one-fifteen before I switched off the light. Some hours later I woke with a start. I sat up in bed, bright as a whistle. I got out and walked to the phone in the hall. I picked up the receiver. There was no message. I thought about calling the police, but I was afraid of getting the same woman again and telling her the same thing. I suppose I was afraid of my embarrassment. So I returned to bed. This time I slept; I slept well. When I woke, sunshine was pouring in the windows. I could hear the TV blabbering away at the other end of the house.

I got up and looked into the spare room in case Stuart had come home in the night and got lost.

It was 11 a.m. before his Subaru wagon pulled up in the drive. I watched from the living-room window. Stuart had on his sunglasses. In the strong morning light he looked pale. I watched him walk towards the front porch. I came out to the hall. I heard him fumble with the key. I could have unlatched the door, but I thought, bugger him. Eventually he got the door open, and as he staggered in I could smell the alcohol on him. His shirt was torn. There was a nasty scratch on his cheek.

'I feel sick,' he said.

For a moment I thought he might mean something else but, no, he leant against the wall rubbing his head, his other hand on his stomach.

'It's eleven o'clock on Sunday morning,' I said.

He held up a hand—to stop me.

'I'm sorry,' he said. 'I'm really sorry. The night just got away on me.'

The night just got away on me. What a wonderful expression that is. Like it was the night's fault. The night was a bull he'd wrestled with and finally submitted to, but not without a fight. Is this what he meant?

Still, I was surprised by my own calm. I said, 'What do you need? Coffee?'

'No. No. Jesus, no,' he said. He waved a soggy arm at me.

I ran him a bath and helped him out of his clothes. In the bath he lay back like a man dying. I got a cold cloth and held it against his forehead. I wondered about the scratch on his cheek. A red crescent tapering off to broken skin. A proper fight and there would have been bruising. A fight with a man, that is. It's funny, isn't it, where your thoughts lead you? Not in a million years would I have thought that one day I would be led down that dark path by a scratch on my husband's cheek. I handed him two disprin and a glass of lemonade. I watched him gulp down the disprin, and sip at the lemonade. I waited, but nothing more was said.

I went out to the front room. I switched off the TV and sent the girls outside. Then I went into the bedroom and closed the curtains. A moment later Stuart came out to the hall, a towel around him. He saw me staring at that scratch. He said, 'It's not what you think it is.' But that's all he said. He said he needed to sleep. He would explain all later.

Bella was due at a friend's birthday party in an hour. I ran down to the bookshop and picked up a gift, then I dropped her off on the other side of the city and left Clara at my sister's.

When I got home Stuart was up. He was in the kitchen waiting for the jug to boil. As I came in he barely looked up. I pulled up a chair and sat down. 'Okay,' he said, 'this is what happened.'

After the office, the younger ones had wanted to go to one of the bars. Stuart and Don had lamely followed.

Stuart is forty-one years old and Don is perhaps a year or two older. I am thirty-seven. The other engineers who'd flown up from the South Island for their 'conference' are younger still. According to Stuart the younger ones led the charge. And one thing led to another. Or, more true to say, one bar led to another.

Around eleven o'clock it occurred to Stuart to ask the others where they were staying. Well, that was the funniest thing, according to Stuart. It seemed none of them had stopped to think that far ahead, so Stuart led them to a backpackers, where the engineers checked in their bags before heading back out to the bright lights.

It seems . . . well, it doesn't seem so much as it happened . . . they headed off to a well-known strip club. This wasn't so much a surprise, I have to say, as Stuart admitting to it; as a result I feel able to trust the rest of what he had to say.

At the strip club, one or two or more, god knows, paid for lap dances. It doesn't matter who, though Stuart did mention names, but a few of them headed upstairs to pay for a woman. That's when I found myself looking back at the scratch on Stuart's cheek.

'So. That's it?' I asked.

'More or less,' he said.

'You spent the whole night in the strip club?'

'No. They did. I didn't.'

Stuart said he left them; he doesn't know what hour that was. He'd had enough, he said. He says he couldn't remember where he'd left the car, which is a good thing. And he'd forgotten about the room he'd paid for at the backpackers. He says he didn't have any idea where he was headed. It was late, but not that late, he claims. Anyway, he says there were still lines of people waiting to get inside the more popular night spots.

Within a block he'd left behind the noise and the lights and the crowds. He was on one of the streets running down to Te Papa on the waterfront. His legs carried him on. He says there was no decision in his head or will left in his body except for in his legs, apparently. Somehow he got himself across those lanes of traffic on Wakefield. I shudder to think. Then, he says, he walked around to the seaward side of the national museum and that's when he saw the flax bushes. As soon as he saw them, he says he knew what to do. He crawled into the flax, where I suppose he passed the rest of the night and which, I gather, accounts for his torn shirt and the cut on his cheek.

In the morning, as he woke in the flax bushes, he says he became aware of others—drunks, I suppose, hoboes, I guess, whatever you wish to call them, street people. That's the company he kept that night sleeping in the flax bushes outside the national museum.

Now, if someone else was telling this story, in other words if all this was being recounted by someone else and it involved someone else's husband and family, I wouldn't know what would have appalled me the most. The lack of a phone call—at any time that night. The binge drinking. The strip club. The lap dancers, or the business upstairs in the strip club. But no, the thing that distresses me the most is the thought of Stuart crawling into those flax bushes. It is the thought of the man I married in good faith waking in the flax bushes with all the other drunks of the city, and it is also this: he is really no better than them, and that fact would be known to everyone if he didn't have a home to go to.

Sunday night I ironed a fresh shirt and left it on the bed. Monday morning I dropped Stuart off at the office for an early meeting with a client. Later I went along to Te Papa as a parent helper with Clara's Year 8 class. It is that time of year when teachers cast around for activities outside the classroom. We took in the Maori waka, and after that the kids scattered and flew like moths to the voices of piped history in various parts of the museum. The trip ended up on the marae level overlooking the waterfront. From there I could look down to the flax bushes where my husband had spent Saturday night.

Already it felt like history. And here I suppose this story might have ended. I might try to forget it, and move on, as everyone says. But while standing there with the rude wind in my face, I felt a nagging that had nothing to do with it or the cries of squabbling children over my shoulder. I decided to take myself down to those flax bushes.

A woman office worker sat on the lawn, smoking and sunning her bare legs while she tackled the crossword. She didn't pay me any attention, though. She didn't see an anxious middle-aged swamphen creep into the shrub and the flax. It was easy to see where people had burrowed through. The ground was well trampled. I poked around. You could see where sleeping bodies had lain, and in one or two places there were plastic and glass bottles lying among the bark chips. One of the other women, the mother of one of Clara's friends, yelled out to me. What was I doing down there? What on earth was I grubbing about for? I could hear her laughing voice rallying above the gusting wind. But I pretended not to hear, and went on looking for a piece of Stuart's white shirt.

The daub of brown paint will be Alice's first building, and working with a quick brush hand Pioneer Towers is up in a jiff. Other than the Towers the surrounding countryside is of a marigold colour, cowlick fields swept back by a steady nor'-wester to the Alps in the west. And just coming onto the canvas—now—is Harry Wills, an Englishman, on the hop from Sydney, whipping his horses across the plains for the Towers. It is late in the day when he draws back the string on his covered wagon. He offers up a hand to his entertainers and they descend and pick their way in gold braid shoes across a muddy street for the new Harold Wills Theatre. It is, as it appears to be, a pale memory, a penny-pinched version of the Globe—not with the same reek of history, of course, but Alice has mixed in some yellow with brown for a weathered look, and stroked in the new/old theatre next to Pioneer Towers. And after the theatre, she plans an eating house and, next to it, a bar, and across the street a police station and gaol. And at the end of the street, a church of sharp cheekbones and high forehead.

Within view of the church Alice adds the farmhouse. A man with a black bag tethers his horse. George Burt, the district veterinarian, has arrived to deliver Alice's mother, and sew up her grandmother, and make her respectable in death. Towards the top of the painting, near the snowline, Alice sketches in a stone farmhouse, to get to which, many years earlier, George Burt rode a day and a night to deliver Alice's father.

And here, on the edge of town, Alice adds the Memorial Hall. On New Year's Eve her father and mother will escape from here into the nearby paddocks. The high-country boy will prod about in the underclothing of Alice's mother, and less than six months later he will be found twitching nervously in the registry room of Pioneer Towers with its official odour of ink and wood. Through the open door he will cast an eye out to the street where the horses stand flicking the wind from their ears. There he will stand then, curling his toes inside his boots. He is twenty-two years old—old enough, he feels, to be irritated by the sense of truancy entering into what is supposedly an honourable act. In two hours' time he and Alice's mother will be making their way to Christchurch for the 'honeymoon', a place from which, instinctively, they know there is no return and of which they can hardly bear to speak.

Alice steps back from the canvas, and pulls a face at the muddy town. The details are too large; they need to be scaled down. A few derelict fence posts are needed to lie in the tall grass, a few sagging lines for the church. And perhaps a memorial clock ought to be grafted on to Pioneer Towers for the farmers' sons who have failed to return.

It also occurs to Alice that sadly there is nothing here for her son, Mark, to recognise or latch on to, except to recall perhaps what a boyish eye once caught from the window of a speeding car. Bless him. Bless my boy and make him grow, Alice says to that part of the canvas, the foreground, which is more familiar.

The scratchy whites and blues are the makeshift shops with their backs to the sea—she can add the details later, because here is the small primary school outside town, where Alice taught and her son attended.

And nearby is their home, a cottage, and in the backyard a woman paints at an easel.

Mark is eight years old, and his father has just bought a cray boat. There will be none of the weekend trips or picnics along the coast they had promised each other before packing up house in Christchurch. The cray boat is no pleasure craft. Nor does the fishing timetable respect weekends. To their friends back in the city they boast of a full life, and too little time. Soon there will be no reply, as many of their friends move overseas, or marry, spawning into streams of their own making. The names are on the tip of Alice's tongue, but the owners' faces have drifted, and parted company with the bits and pieces of Alice's memory.

A number of their friends did make it to Richard's funeral. From others, overseas, came letters and cards of condolence—and a few with chiding tendencies spoke of the 'enormous perils faced by those who *choose* to make their living from the sea', as if Richard had willed the storm—and the boat onto the reef. But there had been kind invitations, too. Summers spent in holiday baches, which she took up for Mark's sake—to give him a nice memory. That is exactly how Alice thought of it, at the time—the opportunity in later life to recall his feet and toes sinking into sand, a moment's premonition of the earth's undertow joyfully ignored, and even shrieked at. But, notably, the first summer Alice decided to stay at home put an end to further invitations.

She created instead summer holidays in the place where they lived. They set up day camps on the sheltered side of the house, and spent all their time between here and the kitchen. At night hot nor'-westers swept down on the town. The wind bellowed in the chimney and the boy climbed into Alice's bed. In the morning they woke to white clouds running with blind terror. One morning Mark asked her to paint the wind. In a whimsical moment she hurled the jar of grey watercolour over the fence at the beach end of the garden. The paint streaked—then briefly rippled as a gust caught underneath and carried it aloft. A day later it formed a dead skin over a small area of dry scrub and beach shingle—and the wind had gone. In a contrite mood the sea straggled ashore in what would be a day of pleasant surprises. Alice set up the easel for Mark in front of the white Peace rose climbing the trellis against the house; she later returned to find among the painted white flower-heads a splash of black and gold. From Mark's canvas she traced the rogue colour on the Peace climber, and gleefully announced, 'A sport.'

She explained to the small boy the aberrant nature of sports, this capacity of a completely different kind of rose to spring unexpectedly from the parent. A sport was outside history. There was no patiently evolved process, no careful layering or natural selection. It just suddenly appeared as its own idea —extraordinary as a new technology or a whole new language. 'Now we get to name it,' she told him. He was in a restless mood. She wasn't even sure he had been listening.

'Call it "no-name rose",' he said.

Alice's paintbrush returns to the school, fleshing out the temporary prefabs that have stayed on, permanently, a flash of silver for the jungle-gym bar on which Mark once split his lip and ran into the staffroom, blood pouring from his mouth.

The painting, she has decided, ought to hang on the wall above the dining-room table. Alice has in mind those whitewashed walls in the photograph Mark sent of his apartment. She imagines him escorting a young woman around the landscape, imagines them arm in arm, stopping at the playground for a turn on the swings. She imagines the three of them going out for breakfast in town—and, for all his acquired foreignness, Mark delighting in his local knowledge. Of course the young woman will not be able to help herself, sniggering with Mark at the powdered coffee, the painted placemats of great thoroughbreds.

Above the town Alice paints the cemetery. She had been happy to bury Richard here, with its lovely views of the bay. She can remember coming here as a family—just the three of them—and Richard kneeling down to whisper in a small boy's ear. 'On a clear day, you can see South America and the peaks of the Andes. On especially clear days, you can see the back of your own head.' On that occasion Mark had looked carefully, squinting his eyes up ambitiously—he'd been about to announce a distant landfall when his father, holding back his laughter, placed his hand over the boy's mouth.

In the weeks after Alice buried Richard she would sometimes spend an hour sitting next to his grave, watching the last of the day depart. One time she measured her own grave—six paces by three—next to Richard's, and sat there, wondering which memories she ought to take with her. And wondering too at the brilliant sunset—is all this simply for me, my benefit alone? Why aren't more people around to enjoy it?

Alice paints her way down from the cemetery through the north end of town towards the railway station. She paints a figure hauling a suitcase, although on the day in question she had driven Mark to the railway station. He had come home simply to say he was leaving. An offer of a job had come from an architect in Sydney.

The two days he was home he refused to go out, afraid of who he might bump into. Finally it was time for Mark to catch the train to Christchurch. Alice drove her son to the station. The entire way, Mark looked out a side window. Perhaps, she thought, he'd been making his own last-minute selections: allowing bits of the town to stick to his wandering gaze to take with him across the Tasman.

There was the matter of her parting gift. She had had to dash back to the car. A 1955 issue of *Pictorial New Zealand*. She shouted through a half-closed window in his carriage, 'It isn't supposed to be reading material. Although, of course, you can read it.'

Rita Hayworth, the Hollywood starlet, was featured that month. There she was with her new husband, Dick, and her two small children, Yasmin and Rebecca, eating breakfast, and Rita has leant across to say something vital and interesting to Dick, all ears with a spoon of cereal poised before his lips. This was the magazine Alice had read in the maternity wing while Mark slept alongside. She had held on to the magazine for reasons that evaded her now. There was another story about Haydn's head being finally returned to the rest of his body, with quite a ceremony in attendance. A priest in sunglasses oversaw the business end, a solemn Italian sculptor bowed over the composer's open casket and in the background of the photograph there were flash-bulbs from the press photographers. Elsewhere in the magazine was another severed-head story—this time a photograph of the tree on which Carl Sylvius Volkner had been strung up, before being dragged by Hauhau rebels into the church, where his head was removed and his blood drunk from a chalice. In the Lifestyle section were tranquil scenes of Milford Sound, night bowls in Parnell; in Dunedin a dog sat patiently outside a butcher's.

Driving home again, Alice had laughed long and hard at the thought of poor Mark opening up the magazine and wondering which of the stories his mother had marked for his attention. Perhaps all she had meant by the gift was that he had arrived at a cer-tain time and place. He shouldn't read too much into it: a dog waiting outside a Dunedin butcher's shop, for instance.

It had been in Mark's later years, those summers he had come home from university, that Alice felt his dis-appointment. It clung to him like an illness. From the hallway she spied on her son as he lay on his bed, wide awake, arms folded beneath his head. And, listening to what he heard, Alice too felt the incompleteness, felt his need to be awed, and at that moment she had understood how this yearning for a real city came close to grief.

But then, as she watched from the hallway and plumbed her son's daydreaming, Alice had been astounded to find him seeding the Canterbury Plains with glass towers and shopping malls, buildings with crested eagles on top, lifts that ran up tower blocks like lit glass balls, and atriums filled with silver trees and tame Amazon parrots.

Alice steps back from the canvas and only now, years later, is it clear to her the space her son's phantom city has occupied. She leans forward, and with her forefinger touches the paint of a tree doubled over from the wind. She finds it hard and dry.

Now, reaching for her paintbrush, Alice begins to reconstruct the tree into something tall and straight and the colour of silver. Now Alice drifts across the city and paints over the empty Theosophical Society building a modern office tower of granite and black glass. Where George Burt delivered her mother, Alice creates a large hospital. A block away, she paints a skyscraper that rises majestically and com-petitively with the Alps. Between this point on the canvas and the old theosophists' meeting place, Alice sets about laying down a mesh of shadowed streets and corner pavements splashed with sunlight and lunchtime crowds. She adds in theatres, restaurants, taverns, and in the midst of this city, this phantom city of Mark's longing, Alice allows for a pocket handkerchief of a park where frisbees float over meadows and young couples lie stapled together. She allows the funny old Colonial replica of the Globe to remain, but over the Harry Wills Theatre she paints the words 'Restaurant and Museum'—outside its doors, a daub of black for the busker, gold for the trombone.

At the port end of town, quite near the stone steps cut into the wharf where Richard once hoisted up his boatloads of cray, Alice places an opera house and, near it, a fish restaurant and an aquarium filled with per-forming dolphins and seals for the tourists. Milling among the crowd over the 'historic' flagstone area are hotdog vendors, jugglers, pickpockets, thieves of all descriptions. There are yellow cabs, policemen on horseback, a flotilla carrying a beauty-pageant queen. There are marching girls, all with their heads tilted in the same direction. A gunman draws back a curtain in a high-up window masked by a blaze of reflected sunlight. Along another darker canyon there is a candle-lit procession. Over the church hovers Alice's paintbrush. She hesitates to demolish it because the city will need a soup kitchen for the lives stranded short of the promised land.

Among a cluster of city buildings, she sees one particular striving tower and is about to add a spire when, to her surprise, Alice recognises the Empire State Building. And here, too, is the Chrysler Building with its distinctive gold-chromed capital. And those tenement buildings—from where did they spring? Now she notices the maple trees in what can only be Central Park. When the paintbrush slides from her fingers she does not bother to pick it up. It can wait. She stares at her painting—not quite able to believe what she has done. Up until now she believed this place to be her own sovereign territory. She realises something else as well. Something equally disheartening. She has found out her son. She has located his dreams. Now she picks up her paintbrush and returns to her plagiarised city. This time her eye is drawn to a small inconclusive feature. She can just see a couple of flecks of black and gold outside the old Harry Wills Theatre—and if she squeezes her eyes tight she can make out the beginnings of something quite new and vital ... She will give the canvas another hour to dry, by which time she will have worked up her base, and then she will start on the no-name rose. She wonders if her son will remember.

Sometimes they held hands, but not very often. As far as Mr Simpson was concerned holding hands was ridiculous, and his wife knew well enough how it irritated him. But when the bus had left the border to enter Russia and Maggie took her husband's hand, there was no attempt to wrestle it away. The Simpsons were on their way to Leningrad. At the thought of which Mr Simpson managed a smile: Leningrad, and the idea of taking a bus there. On two occasions he had taken an intercity bus—once, while work was being done on the car; and another time, after Wellington airport was fogged in, he had bussed up to Palmerston North. But Leningrad could not be mentioned in the same breath as these other times of inconvenience. Great armies had marched on Leningrad.

It was Maggie who had planned the trip. Two weeks ago Mr Simpson was reading the Sunday papers in Holland Park and Maggie had asked if he would like an ice-cream. She left him sitting on the bench for rather a long time; at least, it had seemed that way as the sun faded over the city into a bank of cloud. Picnickers reached for pullovers; Mr Simpson rubbed his bare arms. Frankly it was irritating to wait that long, particularly so when he viewed his wife returning across a field empty-handed. She hadn't been able to find an ice-cream vendor, and Mr Simpson had rolled his eyes: it was ridiculous not to be able to find ice-cream in a park on a Sunday afternoon. His wife had walked all the way to Kensington, where she realised—'silly me,' she said—that an ice-cream would not survive the return journey. This was the news she returned with, before presenting him with a small cardboard notice. Maggie had found it pinned to a bulletin board in a shop entranceway. The notice— written in both English and possibly Russian—invited 'interested parties' to join a bus tour to Leningrad.

Ice-cream, thought Mr Simpson at the passing scenery in the bus window, and alternatively, So this is Russia. It did not seem like a superpower. There was barely any traffic on the road, and the passing farmland looked unproductive and unkempt. All the same he was glad they were off to Leningrad—and not, say, Rome or Venice or those other postcard cities. The Simpsons didn't know anybody who had been to Leningrad, not even Yvonne, their oldest daughter, who taught English to businessmen in Turkey.

They had to get themselves to Berlin. The rendez-vous was a street corner in the Kreuzberg where the unexpected number of daytime prostitutes, Turks, kebab bars and nightclubs had caused the Simpsons some alarm. Mrs Simpson had needed to push her husband from behind to get him to board the bus. It was her idea. She had to provide the enthusiasm. Put a brave face on things. Out of the bus window, Mr Simpson had watched a young man sit down in a shop doorway, roll up a shirtsleeve and plunge a needle into his arm. Mr Simpson felt a sudden rush of panic; and it was perhaps just as well that the way out was blocked by their fellow passengers humping suitcases and card-board boxes along the aisle. He could smell food, foreign food—the sharp rotten smell of unrefrigerated meat and forgotten cheese. This was the other time on the trip Maggie had reached for his hand and given it a firm squeeze, as if to say, 'Everything will be all right.'

Last night they had driven through Poland. Around

dawn Mr Simpson briefly awoke to discover they were in a city. He thought it might be Warsaw; and he had thought about waking Maggie to say they were in Warsaw, but instead he fell asleep again, and the next time he woke they were travelling in the countryside. It wasn't until the bus had reached the border, or shortly before it, that the Simpsons were given a rest stop.

Tonight they would be in Kaunas; Daugavpils; Riga around dawn, and, late afternoon, Pskov, and Leningrad later that night.

Mr Simpson started a letter to Yvonne. He wrote that they had spent much of the day passing through 'no-account country'. But he fell asleep before he could explain himself.

Shortly before dusk the bus stopped, but not at Kaunas. Mr Simpson had brought a map with him, and he could see they were a short distance east of where the itinerary placed them. Tall pines made a secret of the surrounding countryside. They had stopped at a restaurant and a warm and almost circular glow in the distance suggested they were on the outskirts of a small town.

'Look here,' Mr Simpson said to the Greek driver. 'Shouldn't we be in Kaunas?' The driver gazed at the plastic which covered Mr Simpson's map, then at Mr Simpson with a flicker of contempt for his need to know, as if to say, 'I decide. Me. The driver.' Mr Simpson trailed after him.

He could hear his wife saying, 'I'm sure it is all right. There's no point in our worrying.' Then she said, 'Look, we're the only ones not inside the restaurant.' He turned back to her. Suddenly they could hear voices, and laughter, and even what sounded like tears. Over the windows of the restaurant were wooden shutters and warm glow at the bottom of each sill. It occurred to Mr Simpson that they were the only ones left outside. Alone, out here in the Russian night, thought Mr Simpson. Well, it was not quite night because they could see the tops of the pines. But Mr Simpson thought it might be a moment worth telling about once they got home. It would be something Maggie would bring up. 'Bill, why don't you tell Paddy and Dan about that time in Russia . . .' His wife would have on oven-gloves and she would be holding an oven-hot casserole dish, and he would shoot a quick look of disapproval, or perhaps laugh, as if she had rekindled a lost memory.

They walked along a path of trodden pine-needles. Mr Simpson allowed his hand to be held, but inside the restaurant, in the cloakroom area, he shook free. Through another set of doors a speech was in progress. Mr Simpson braced himself for the moment when a roomful of faces would stare his and Maggie's way; but none did. They pushed through the swing-doors and no one paid the Simpsons the slightest attention. A man with greying hair and a sad drooping moustache was giving the speech. At times he interrupted himself to blow his nose and brush away a tear. Mr Simpson's eyes moved to the far end of the room, where in an open doorway he saw the driver seated at a table. He had started on his food and ate hungrily from a fork, while keeping his other hand on the stem of a wine glass for fear it would be removed, or stolen. None of what was happening in the restaurant seemed to be of concern to him.

There were two long tables set with white table-cloths. Bouquets of wild flowers were set between carafes of spring water. Now, at last, a man in a waist-coat, an older man about Mr Simpson's age, found them a place at the bottom end of the second table. The Simpsons stepped over a bench and sat down. The Russian spoke in Mr Simpson's ear, but it was unintelligible. Mr Simpson spoke in English. He said he was sorry. The waiter shushed him. He held up the palms of his hands, as if Mr Simpson had expressed impatience.

The speech had come to an end, and now the speaker began to read from a list of names. 'Serge.' A man got up from the Simpsons' table. A second name was called. 'Masha.' A woman slowly rose from the other table. The entire room looked up. The man 'Serge' held out his hands and the woman walked over to where he stood, and took both his hands. Another woman at the other table was crying loud, painful sobs. Now the speaker held up his glass and offered a toast and on either side of the Simpsons glasses were raised. The Simpsons tried to follow suit but were raising their own as the rest of the glasses in the room were returned to their resting places. Applause broke out. From both tables people called out 'Masha' and 'Serge'. Room was made at the top end of the Simpsons' table, and the couple sat down. When the woman began to touch the man's face with her fingertips Mr Simpson looked away. He folded his napkin and looked at it a while.

The name 'Andrei' was called out—it was the man who had sat across the aisle on the bus. This morning he had offered Maggie a carrot smeared with horse radish. Mr Simpson had declined it with a wave of his hand. Maggie had smiled, and said, 'No, but thank you very much.' They had their water crackers and tea flask.

Now this same man left the table to run and hug 'Lenka', a woman unused to make-up perhaps, and whose hair was more usually kept in a scarf. The women whose names were called appeared older than the men. Their faces bore the lines of perseverance Mr Simpson had seen in old *National Geographics*—Soviet women in overalls and scarves, shouldering brooms and shovels.

Not everyone stood up and paired off, thankfully. And soon the business was completed, and the Simpsons were fed a watery stew of potatoes and cabbage. The man alongside pointed to the contents of his glass and said, 'Schnapps.' Mr Simpson nodded that he understood. So did Mrs Simpson.

There was no dessert. There were second helpings if the Simpsons cared for them. The other diners, Mr Simpson noted, gave no thought to it; and he did not wish to appear insensitive. The room was abuzz with laughter and had recovered the high spirits of earlier, when the Simpsons had found themselves alone, outside. The 'couples' wandered around the two tables. The women presented their men, who were embraced, their faces held and kissed on both sides.

They were deserters from the Russian army. Soldiers in the last regiments to fall back from occupied Germany in the late forties. Men impatient to be with their girlfriends, their wives and families. They had fled the army, only to flee their homeland.

Mr Simpson learnt this outside the restaurant. Maggie was off trying to find a bathroom; and he was enjoying a cigarette when he felt a tap on his shoulder, and the surprise of his name spoken.

'Mr Simpson, please?'

It was the same man who had shown them to their place in the restaurant. Over his shoulder Mr Simpson saw the doors of the restaurant burst open with the exit of a happy laughing couple and there was a split-second view of the bus driver looking back his way.

The man in the waistcoat was very polite. He meant no harm. But he needed to know some things.

'How did you find this bus tour, please?'

Mr Simpson told him the business of his wife going out to buy ice-cream—how she had returned with the cardboard notice. And the man said, 'Yes, yes,' as if these were things he already knew. He said there was a man, Kolya, and he pointed back at the restaurant. Kolya had a confectionary shop popular with Russian émigrés in London. Could it have been there that Mr Simpson's wife had found the notice?

'Look, she went out to buy ice-cream. That's all,' said Mr Simpson. He didn't know anything about Russian deserters. He told the man he was a builder. A successful builder. Then he told him the name of his country, as if that fact alone might explain everything.

'It is very important,' the man said. 'The women are to travel in the bus as far as Leningrad. From there they will return and the men will carry on. Please, we do not want unhappiness. We wish to avoid mistakes.' The man asked Mr Simpson to show mercy. 'These people are not traitors. They are husbands and wives.'

There were more people than seats on the bus but no one thought to complain. Mr Simpson looked out the window. It was pitch-black. Nowhere did there appear so much as a farmhouse light. He guessed they would be on back roads all the way to Leningrad. He passed on to Maggie what he had been told. He whispered of the people around them who were swaying in the bus aisle, laughing and kissing. Someone had a camera and was taking photographs. Across the aisle Lenka sat in Andrei's lap. He tickled her behind the ear, and she in turn gave his nose a playful tweak. A Polaroid was passed around. The couple laughed at themselves in the photo. Only in the photograph did Mr Simpson notice the woman's bad teeth. She was laughing and he could see the black pits of her teeth and the swollen gums.

Here were people—men and women the Simpsons' age—laughing and crying. There was a jokester among them—a man with a shaven head and twinkling blue

eyes who every so often rose out of his seat and shouted
something that cracked everyone up at the Simpsons'
end of the bus. To the front of the bus were younger
faces—young men and women—and Mr Simpson
wondered if they were relations, perhaps even the off-
spring of marriages forged in newly adopted countries.

Mr Simpson looked at his watch, as was his custom
before turning off the bedside light. It was ten o'clock
when he sealed his face with a smile and closed his eyes.
He never really managed to fall asleep. The bus rocked
and on corners pitched him sideways. When next he
opened his eyes the lights in the bus were out. It was
quiet. Maggie was sitting upright, wide awake but lost
in thought. Mr Simpson had to shake her arm to make
her aware that he was no longer asleep. He said he
would like a peppermint. Maggie felt around in a bag
for the peppermints. The rustling of the peppermint
bag was unreasonably loud, like in a picture theatre,
and Mr Simpson was suddenly aware of the other
noises.

Across the aisle in the tight confines of their seat,
Andrei and Lenka rested awkwardly in each other's
arms. Towards the back of the bus, in the aisle, a man
lay on top of a woman who still had her shoes on.

Once, many years ago, Mr Simpson and Maggie
had made love on the floor of a bach—and an hour

later sat in the same spot with the Ralstons eating a ham salad.

Mr Simpson took a peppermint from his wife, and popped it in his mouth. He noted Maggie's restlessness, a certain look that overtook her face when he occasionally breached a rule of etiquette, and wondered if it was the noise of him sucking the peppermint. Then she whispered, 'Have you noticed?' Yes, he nodded. He had noticed. 'Those poor people,' she whispered. She felt that they should give up their seat.

'For the time being. We can do that at least,' she said, and she gave a slight nod for Mr Simpson to check the aisle behind.

Two couples were embracing. Mr Simpson reached across to the nearest pair and tapped the man on the trouser leg. The man lifted his foot and shook his leg, and went on kissing the woman. This time Mr Simpson pulled on the man's coat, and was more successful.

A man with grey sideburns and crew-cut turned around. He was perhaps a few years Mr Simpson's junior, but he had held and continued to hold his woman like a teenager, both hands around her waist, her crotch pulled in against his own. Mr Simpson might have thought of the time he switched on a light to surprise his daughter with Grant Wicks. But there was no such terror in the eyes of the Russian man—not even surprise. More a patient kind of curiosity. But the woman understood before he did and gave a big smile and a push when she saw Mr Simpson and his wife stand up from their seat.

The Russian man clasped Mr Simpson by the shoulders and nodded formally. Mr Simpson gave the man a pat on the shoulder. Maggie was smiling happily. She felt proud; and Mr Simpson knew that part of that pride was for himself. He knew he had done something that his wife would never have expected him to do.

'Hold me,' she said. Mr Simpson did what was asked of him. Mrs Simpson put her hands against his chest, to steady herself, and then rested her head there. They stayed like that for a few minutes; then his wife looked up. She wanted him to kiss her. Mr Simpson wiped his mouth with the back of his hand and cleared his throat, as if he was about to deliver a few words, and kissed his wife.

'That was nice,' she said, and put her head back against his chest.

Mr Simpson was watching the Russian couple making love on their seat, and he was wondering what he and Maggie would look like. He watched the heave of the man's body—and the woman's mouth open to catch bubbles of air. The expertise in the man's limbs caused Mr Simpson to wonder if he would appear the same, and whether after such a long separation from Maggie he would be able to restrain the greed of his body, and how could one sustain the greed without the separation?

Once he had thought about leaving Mrs Simpson. It was after the birth of their second child, and Mr Simpson had started to think about other women. It turned out to be a passing thing. And, of course, he had never told Maggie. Now he turned his thoughts to the young faces in the front of the bus. And as he watched he wondered which life the Russian man was thinking of, at that particular moment.

All of a sudden the motion stopped. The man's head fell to one side; the woman's eyes opened and smiled at Mr Simpson. Maggie crouched down and scratched around in her bag until she found the bottle of Vittel. She poured a cup and handed it to the woman, who had to reach over the man's shoulder to receive it.

'Spasiba,' she said.

The man whispered something, and the woman said in hesitant English, 'Thank you.'

She kissed the man's forehead and gently pushed him up, and as he reluctantly rose he pulled up his trousers, and the woman flicked her coat over her legs.

She slapped the seat beside her, rose, and said something in Russian. The man agreed.

'Yes,' he said and, nodding at the Simpsons, gestured to the space left behind.

Mrs Simpson laughed. 'Oh no,' she said. Then she smiled up at her husband. Mr Simpson rested a hand on his wife's hip. The other couple moved away. The man patted Mr Simpson's cheek with his hand. Mr and Mrs Simpson resumed their seat.

'I feel so . . .' she began to say, but Mr Simpson cut off the sentence with his lips. For a moment he wondered how things would appear in the morning and, back home, what he and Maggie would tell their friends. Then he felt inside his wife's coat for her breast, and discovered the nipple ready.

where the harleys live

A group of them had been swapping stories about their parents: about life growing up under other people. Harley had told a story about his father, the ritual surrounding the family car, and the way his mother had driven the old man everywhere. His father was a big man, in the physical sense, who wore buttoned-up cardigans. He hardly ever spoke, and sat with his hands folded in his lap, while his wife drove him to the Phillips plant, to the bowling club, and home from the RSA. On Friday evenings she would lead him up the path to the house, quietly guiding him at the elbow, and, despite the gallons of alcohol slurping around inside of him, there was always a terribly serious look on his father's face.

Easterman told how it had been necessary to lie to his elderly grandmother, and tell her he was marrying a Catholic. He had married a dental nurse, Karen. They married at Our Lady of Mercy. There is a photo on the Eastermans' wall. Mark in his number ones, Karen in white, there they are smiling down at the crowd gathered on the steps of the church. Karen appears to be touchingly surprised by the crowd that has turned out. Easterman, on the other hand—you sense he is about to reach for his speech notes.

It was later at that same party that Easterman drew Harley aside to tell how he had fallen for Mary-Anne Richmond. 'Does she know?' Harley asked—without intending the insult. The Richmonds he had known for years. Terry Richmond was in Japan to sew up a deal with a rubber-technology plant to bring in a hard-wearing synthetic rubber. He ran a small factory further up the line, a large tin-roofed warehouse in a paddock, turning out shoe soles. As for Mary-Anne, she had a useful profile about town. She was always out and about, getting involved with things. She was someone you called when you needed someone to knock on doors. There was a time when she marched around the car park of the supermarket with her placard of support for the Sandinistas. The Harleys knew her through the play centre, and of course Mary-Anne was a force behind the community theatre.

Towards the end of winter she had telephoned to badger Harley to take part in the local production. 'Not this year, but maybe next year, Mary-Anne,' he said, which was the same answer he had given the previous year, and the year before that. 'Well,' she said, 'I've got your name down for backstage, to help with the curtains and lighting on one of the nights—that okay?' Harley said it was, in the safe knowledge he would not be required.

Two months earlier Easterman had got the same call, and actually turned up at the auditions for a school fundraiser, *Sleeping Beauty*.

Apparently he and Karen were going through a sticky patch. At least this was the account Easterman gave Harley. He just wanted something that would get him out of the house. So he went along to the school hall and landed the part of the Prince, who comes across the sleeping Kingdom—and awakens it and the Princess with a perfectly delivered kiss.

Come audition time, Easterman had wandered out to the middle of the stage. He raised his hand against the glare of the stage footlights and said he was sorry, but he had nothing prepared; however, he would sing 'Jerusalem' if required. Everyone fell about laughing.

Easterman hadn't intended a joke, but was pleased anyway, and grinned back in the direction of the darkened hall.

His next time on stage Easterman waved his arms through an imaginary thicket of undergrowth and cobwebs to where Mary-Anne Richmond lay asleep. Easterman knelt beside the Princess, imparted a trusting look to the audience, then lowered his lips against Mary-Anne Richmond's. To Easterman's surprise, the kiss lingered, and the Princess offered a murmur of satisfaction.

Later, after the show, Easterman picked up his five-year-old boy and held him in his arms, and while his wife was saying, 'You were great. Wonderful. Really. Wasn't he, Paulie?' he looked around for the Princess.

The second show passed uneventfully. Easterman knelt down and delivered the kiss, which he said was once again received with the same willingness. But later, when the cast and audience mingled, he couldn't find the Princess. He hung about until he was reasonably sure that she had left, and went home.

The final night there was to be a party for the cast, and partners, at the house of the director, Simon Bragg. A few days before, Easterman had told Karen he wasn't interested; three nights on the trot had left him sapped to the bone, and he was ready for an early night. Then, at the last moment, when it was too late to arrange a babysitter, Easterman had come home from work, complaining about the choice being out of his hands. He'd been rung at work. Everyone, and especially Bragg, expected the Prince to be there.

So Easterman read bedtime stories to his kids, turned out the lights, and eased into his green tights, suede calf-high boots and ruffled shirt. Karen handed him his sword at the door, and Easterman drove off to the final performance and, later, the party at Bragg's.

When he came through the director's house he could see the Princess's bonnet above the party crowd on the back lawn. Small flames flickered from kerosene-soaked flints on the end of bamboo poles, and as some dreadful old, bent hag pushed a cup of mulled wine into his hands he looked again and recognised Edith Saunders from the Plant Centre. The others, however, remained strangers. Peasants. Dwarves. Cobblers. Blacksmiths. Witches.

He tried to attach himself to the Princess's group. They were talking politics. One of the Witches and the Woodsman—a former Treasury man it turned out—spoke familiarly about politicians whose names Easterman recognised from the newspaper. The Princess held a cigarette. She maintained a wry smile, which Easterman hoped was for him, although discouragingly her eye discreetly flitted between the Woodsman and the Witch. Easterman made a couple of trips to the bar. The third or fourth time he returned to find the group disbanded, and the Princess alone.

She smiled at him.

'Well,' she said, and tripped forward on the word just enough to surprise Easterman. She had obviously been drinking. 'Are you still my handsome Prince?' She was holding her cigarette upwards like a film actress and, ever so slightly, swaying on her feet. Easterman said he was, and gulped down his wine. The Princess looked at her own glass, then, nodding at Easterman's, said, 'I could use one of those.'

Some of the cast had moved inside the house to play charades. One of the Courtiers was on his back kicking his white tights in the air.

'Crab!' someone yelled.

'A dying frog!'

Easterman filled the glasses from the cask, and closed the tap. When he returned to the lawn the Princess was gone—and he stood there in that flickering darkness holding the two glasses. He was beginning to feel foolish. He was thinking he would tip the wine into the flax bushes and head home when he saw the lit end of a cigarette. The deck was below the back lawn and jutted out from the hillside. He found the narrow path at the side of the lawn, and as soon as he stepped onto the deck the Princess turned and stubbed out her cigarette and moved inside his arms, and Easterman, with each hand holding a wine glass, was marched backwards until he was pinned against the balcony, and the woman's mouth clamped on to his.

Harley had just arrived at the shop when the phone rang. It was Easterman saying it was urgent that he see him—'About last night.'

'Oh that.' And he proceeded to tell Easterman he needn't worry.

There was a brief pause, and then Easterman said, 'Why should I worry? Listen. This is important. I want you to meet me at the gardens. If that's convenient.'

'Sure. The Municipal Gardens.'

'Good. That's good. Now listen, can you walk there? I'll explain later. Oh, and make it twelve-fifteen, no later. That's okay?'

It meant Harley had to call in Giddy to cover the lunch hour. The wine-trail bus was scheduled to come through at one-fifteen. The bus would stop at the tea rooms. They could usually count on a small number trickling down the road to investigate the antiques sign. Last year he sold a dozen horseshoes to an

American. He immediately got in another dozen horseshoes but they had sat there ever since.

He told Giddy he should be back in time for the bus.

'I hope so,' she said. 'I dropped Robbie off at Karen's. I don't want to leave him too long. What's it all about?'

'Easterman. I don't know. He rang before, sounding like his house roof was on fire.'

He was rather pleased Easterman had called. It was nice to be outside. He could feel the sun on his neck. He would have brought his sunglasses had he thought there was a need. There was hardly any breeze and the leaves shone with newness on the line of oaks at the edge of the gardens. There was Easterman in sunglasses leaning against the fender of his Commodore. He looked preoccupied. Scattered over the grass were people who had walked down from town to eat their lunch. The girls who worked in the bank sat near the rose beds, spooning yoghurt. They looked heartbreakingly fragile. They were not so long out of school uniform, but already their skin had lost its healthy all-year-round sheen. They had become constrained and a little lifeless. Behind their tills in the bank they all looked and sounded the same—'How are we today, Mr Harley?' Their parents ran the local businesses. Most of them he knew.

Easterman made a thing of consulting his watch.

'You're late,' he said.

'Customers,' Harley said, getting into the passenger side. He wound down the window. It was that sort of day. As they drove by the end of the gardens he could hear the sounds of splashing from the swimming pool beside the gardens; the shrieks, and the loose creaking of the diving board. He'd racked his brains these past months for another line of revenue. Those sorts of problems could blind you. He had missed the things he usually liked to think about at this time of the year. It occurred to him he was getting fat.

They were driving away from town towards the ranges. At some point he expected they would turn north or south and run along the flats behind town.

Easterman changed down for the last intersection. He said, 'I'll explain as we go.'

A kilometre south of the macrocarpa windbreak on the corner of Hilltops Road that runs back to town, Easterman eased on the brakes. The Commodore slid on the loose metal until it came to a halt on the shoulder. He left the motor running and sprang the boot. Harley couldn't see Easterman in the back window for the raised lid, but he heard him call out, 'You drive.'

Harley slid over to the driver's side. The seat was still moist from Easterman. He heard the boot slam down, and then the back passenger door opened—and Easterman climbed in wearing the Prince costume.

'Okay, we're late. Let's go.'

'Go where?'

'Christ. Where the hell do you think?'

Harley pushed on the gas.

'It's her idea. Really, I don't care either way. She gets off on the Prince and Princess thing.'

Near the macrocarpas Easterman said, 'You probably think it a bit kinky?' He gave an unconvincing laugh. 'Come on, Dave,' he said. 'Lighten up.'

Hilltops Road is long and straight. It runs between the western ranges and the small, white shopfronts in town. On Saturday nights cars race up and down here. Once, Harley and Rex Kirby out on a Sunday-morning run had stopped to inspect a farm ute, lying on its side in a field of young corn. The driver turned out to be a twelve-year-old; his father, a sharemilker, was in bed asleep by eight o'clock and never knew the vehicle was gone. In other circumstances Harley might have passed this incident on to Easterman. The exact spot drew up and then receded in the rear mirror. It had been the Eastermans who bought the Kirby house, and before leaving the district the Kirbys had hosted a lunch to introduce the Eastermans to the neighbourhood.

Thinking back to last night there were any number

of times he could have said 'enough' to Easterman. He could have stopped the story in its tracks. But for most of it he couldn't believe what he was hearing. And quite sincerely he wished it was someone else, not Mary-Anne. She would be appalled to know of his involvement. And despite Easterman's assurances he was sure she would find out, then inevitably she would move to distance herself. Probably she would not call again to tempt him in the local production. He would miss that.

'Listen,' said Easterman, 'do you like Ray Charles? In the dash there you'll find the tapes. The other stuff is Karen's. I don't know if you like that stuff or not.'

Then, from his prone position on the back seat, Easterman said all over again how much he and Mary-Anne appreciated what Harley was doing here to help out.

'So Mary-Anne knows about me knowing?'

'No. Not exactly,' said Easterman. 'We had thought about a taxi but didn't think it sensible. I told her to leave it with me. I would think of something.'

'That's me. A "something",' Harley said.

Easterman said he was a pal. And that it wouldn't go unrewarded.

'No, really,' he said. 'The cash register at the store

can't exactly be ringing its merry head off out here in Nowheresville.'

'Go to hell.'

Easterman laughed. 'Okay. Out of order. Fair enough. But all the same,' he said, and a hand dropped over Dave's shoulder with a fifty-dollar bill. Harley put on the brakes and pulled over to the kerb. They were only half a mile from Mary-Anne's place, and they had stopped. That was it. There was still time to bail out. He would walk back along South Road, past the sun-drenched houses reflected in the rear mirror. He was half out the door when Easterman reached out and pleaded.

'Now, come on. I'm sorry. Okay? No listen, I'm sorry. I really am. I didn't mean to insult you. I didn't realise.'

'Does Mary-Anne know about this?'

'I told you,' he said. 'You've got nothing to worry about. Look at my bloody armpits. She's expecting me. Believe me, Dave, this is it. I promise. After today, no more. Kaput. Anyway her husband gets back Friday.'

'Terry.'

'Yeah. Her husband. What is wrong with you?'

'Her husband's name is Terry.'

'Okay. So Terry gets back on Friday. So Mary-

Anne, she made it clear. Absolutely clear, man. This is it. Now will you close the car door? Please?'

Harley swung his legs inside the door, and Easterman slapped his shoulder.

In the Richmonds' street Easterman asked if anyone was out and about.

'Yeah, there's a brass band outside Mary-Anne's.'

'I just want to be careful.' Then he added, 'For Mary-Anne's sake as much as mine.'

'Everyone is at work or dead.'

'Hey, that's funny. That's how this place struck me the first time.'

Harley ran up the Richmonds' drive. It curled around the end of the house to an area of privacy: bricks, a patch of lawn and a small number of apple and plum trees. Easterman slid out the back door. He knelt by the window.

'One-thirty, okay?' he said. 'You're a pal.'

In town the inside traffic got the green arrow, so Harley switched lanes and ran down to the gardens. He parked where Easterman had, realising as he did that a grubby pattern had been completed. He got out of the car and stood for a moment surveying the scene. The lunch crowd had dispersed. Near the freshly sown cricket block a young man cautiously doubled up and played a defensive stroke with a boundary stick to a delivery made with a balled-up brown paper bag. At the end of the stroke the batsman looked up. He put his hand up to ward off another delivery, waved. It was the Richmonds' oldest boy. Harley waved back. The university term must be over, and Pete had drifted back home for the summer. He watched the Richmonds' boy make his slow and self-aware way towards the car.

'Pete,' he said, shaking him by the hand. Pete had done some work for him one vacation and they had got on well together. He had Mary-Anne's wit and his father's clockmaker's face. It could make for a curious mix—his eyes narrowing up as the mouth yapped on.

Pete said he had dropped by the shop. He and Andrea.

This was Andrea joining them now with the rolled-up paper bag.

'This is Mr Harley,' he said to the girl. 'The antiques store?'

'Oh right,' she said. 'It's nice to meet you.'

They had arrived last night. The nine-o'clock train. And spent the morning walking around town looking for shop work. That sort of thing.

'Actually, it's got to the point where I will do anything at all,' said Andrea. 'I'm here until Christmas.'

'She doesn't want to work in the factory. The blue rinse won't wash out of the genes.'

Pete laughed—his mother's laugh.

'I will and I can,' said Andrea. When she smiled she seemed so much older. 'I would rather not. That's all.'

She rubbed her flat stomach. 'Hunger pangs,' she said.

Pete said, 'We'll head home and eat something and hit the traps after lunch.'

'Home?' Harley said. Pete and Andrea looked at him expectantly. In the next moment, to his surprise, he was offering Andrea work.

The girl couldn't believe her luck, and Pete was saying to her, 'See, what did I tell you?'

'Only part-time, mind you, and it won't pay much,' Harley hastened, but Andrea wasn't the slightest bit discouraged.

'What did I say?' said Pete. He placed his arm around her shoulder and squeezed her tight.

'That's great. Just great, Mr Harley,' he said.

'I'll give you a call, shall I?' said the girl.

The two of them were about to move off.

'Wait. You'll need to see the shop.'

'We have,' said Andrea. 'The umbrella stand made from the horseshoes. Wow.'

Harley gave the girl a bullying look. He placed his hands on his hips.

'Now tell me this,' he said. 'Has this buffoon shown you the sights yet, or just pushed you into shop doorways? Eh?' Then he said, 'Come on, you two. A quick tour is called for. We'll pick something up on the road. What do you say?'

Andrea gave a nervous laugh. She shrugged and looked at Pete.

'Well, I don't know,' said Pete.

Harley kept a stern eye on Andrea, and very deliberately she began to nod her head. She looked at her feet, then at Pete, and smiled.

Pete sat in the front—Andrea in the back. She leant forward to share the view. They followed the road out beyond town, and headed north along the foothills, where there was no traffic. A farmer on a tractor noiselessly motored through a field of young maize. In the rear mirror Harley watched Andrea lift a strand of blonde hair to her face and let it fall over her finger.

'It's so quiet out here,' she said, almost whispering.

'Quiet as quiet can be,' he said.

'I imagine you could hear a pin drop.'

'On occasion,' he said.

'It must be lovely living out here.'

'Lovely and boring,' said Pete. 'If there was a market

for boredom with the monetary value of uranium, we would be the new sheiks. Isn't that right, Mr Harley?'

Andrea brightened at the thought.

'We could can it. One-hundred, two-hundred, and five-hundred gram cans of boredom.'

'Environmentally friendly cans of boredom,' said Pete.

'We could have special bilateral agreements with Poland and Nauru—and where else? Pete?'

'Pitcairn Island. Norway. Iceland. The Falklands.'

He had closed his eyes.

They came to a crossroads up ahead, and turned back for the highway.

'Hotdog Heaven . . . looks like,' Pete told Andrea.

Fries. Hotdogs and mustard. Fresh bread rolls that were not light but soggy. They sat at an outside table. Behind a planted toi-toi the traffic rushed past.

Harley said to Andrea, 'Pete's dad's factory is just five minutes up the road.'

Slightly longer, as it turned out. Pete and Andrea had switched places, and he could sense Andrea's unease at there being nothing on the horizon, no sign of the factory. She would be full of all the questions such a view insists on, about what they were doing here, and where they might be headed. Harley told her he had kids of his own. He thought that might relax her. Robbie, eighteen months. Juliette.

'She will be eight next month. She's crazy about tennis.'

'That's nice. Tennis,' she said, with a serious nod.

At last the SANZ Plastics sign was drawing them off the road and onto the drive—towards a corrugated-iron building.

'Here we are,' he said, and made a small loop in the car park. 'Pete's dad is a big fish around here. The factory employs eighteen people. Eighteen people is it, Pete?'

'Eighteen,' he said.

Harley tried to think of what else to say, about the factory and Pete's father. Some of the parents had stuck together after their kids moved on from the play centre, but quite early on Terry had retired from the group and left the socialising to Mary-Anne. As far as he could recall, no one had ever spoken ill of Terry. Mary-Anne's husband was the gentle retiring presence in the party background, or holding down the quiet and reasoned end of a dinner party. A helluva nice guy, is what people said.

Harley was aware that the three of them were staring at the side of the factory, so he said to Pete, 'So how's tricks with Terry and Mare?'

'Dad's in Japan. Mum? I don't know,' the boy said

wearily. He mentioned his mother's involvement in the local production. 'You know how she gets excited by these things,' he said. *Sleeping Beauty*. It had done well. Full houses. Pete talked on, and Harley wondered how his mother and Easterman were getting on, and whether the Prince and Princess stuff would feature. He wondered if Easterman would bother with a shower afterwards.

'This time around,' Pete was saying, 'the house seems that much smaller, more quiet. And actually, you know, more spooky because of it. I remember home being a sprawling place, and with more rooms. Mum was in more of a hurry.'

'She was always a busy woman. Your mother.'

'When there was a war on.'

'Nicaragua,' Harley laughed. 'Remember that?'

'Nicaragua what?' asked Andrea, and Pete said he would tell her later.

'Well, that's the factory, then,' Harley said.

Andrea turned around to Pete. She smiled and rolled her eyes.

Back on the highway they caught up to the traffic and slowed right down. Harley wound down the window and could hear the strain of the wine bus up ahead trying to hold its place.

The clock on the dash said one-ten. Harley felt more

relaxed. He wouldn't bother with the back route. He would drive straight into town and drop the kids off there. He would pick up Easterman and get back to the shop for the wine bus. He was happily dozing in the slow traffic when Andrea piped up.

'Do you mind if I ask you a personal question?'

'I'm eighty-five kilograms,' Harley said, and from the back Pete laughed. Andrea smiled out the side window—she shook her head, then she turned back to Harley with a broader, goofier smile.

'Okay,' Harley said. He was going to be a real bore and ask each of them what they planned on doing when they had finished up with university.

Andrea turned around to Pete.

'You go first.'

'Andrea wants to go to America,' he said. 'New York. That's right, isn't it, Andrea?'

'Pete wants to go to Australia. Yawn. Excuse me. And work on a shrimp boat.'

The traffic started to move then. The cars in single file moved around the wine bus. Harley managed a quick glance but didn't recognise the driver. Although it might have been Alun Richards. It could have been Alun just wearing sunglasses. He hit the gas and the car shot ahead.

Andrea fell back in her seat. They got round the bus

and fell into line, and Andrea picked up that strand of hair with her fingers again, and twirled it.

Harley apologised. 'I'm sorry. You were going to ask me a question.'

'It was nothing really,' she said. 'I suppose I just want a stimulating life.'

'It's a state of mind,' Pete said.

'That's true, too,' said Harley. But at that moment he had seen in his rear mirror the bus turn off the highway for Owens Bush.

He looked at his watch and couldn't figure out where the bus was headed.

Harley slowed the car onto the shoulder and, finally, made his mind up to stop. The top of the bus could be seen moving across the paddocks, then disappeared altogether, on a diagonal line into the earth.

'Is everything all right?' asked Andrea. Harley didn't reply. He was aware the girl was exchanging anxious looks with her boyfriend.

He turned the car around and shot up the highway and took Owens Bush Road. Usually Alun would take the tourists to Sunkist Orchards, Millars Vineyard and Winery, and move on from there.

He asked Pete and Andrea if they could see anything. Forking off left and right were plenty of farm roads the bus could have taken.

'Is that what we're looking for? A bus?' said Andrea. 'I don't believe this. Now we're looking for a bus?' She turned around to giggle at Pete.

Harley braked and the car slid in the gravel and came to rest. The heat. The dust and splattered yellow gorse flowers gathered outside the window. It was 'sit and wait' air. He got out of the car and climbed onto the hood, and up onto Easterman's rooftop to scan the surrounding farmland. He could see the winery. The front yard was bare. The same front yard where he might expect to have seen a good number of Americans—middle-aged couples, the women with dead-looking hair and the men with leather money-belts and sunglasses, their bored gazes staring across empty paddocks.

They drove in silence. The girl was back to calling him 'Mr Harley'. She said she was sorry about the bus. She hadn't meant to laugh.

'I don't see why not,' said Harley.

Here they were on the back route, passing the spot where Easterman had pulled over to get into his Prince suit. Up on Hilltops Road they passed the place where he and Rex Kirby had discovered the ute in the corn fields. He could hear Pete telling Andrea, 'Billy Terrell was killed there.' He was saying that once, years ago, he and Billy Terrell had built a tree fort together.

They came into the main-road traffic. Harley heard the girl breathe more easily.

She said, 'Well, that was interesting.'

'It's a quiet place,' Pete said.

Harley didn't say anything.

'You've been very kind, Mr Harley,' Andrea said. 'I'm sorry I said that about the bus.'

Harley could see by the look on the girl's face she was worried about whether there was still a job.

They got caught by the light, so Harley asked the girl what the question was she had wanted to ask.

'Oh that . . .' And she reached for the strand of hair. 'It's not important. I was wondering if you ever thought you would end up living here? See, it's a dumb question.'

'No,' Harley said. 'Never.'

A few minutes later, through the glass of the antiques store, he could see his wife dusting the World War One helmets. There was nobody else in the store. Harley said he would drop them off here. He had a quick errand to do. 'Go and say hi to Giddy,' he said to Pete. He looked back in the window and met his wife's questioning glance. She was looking at Easterman's car. He doubted she knew the Commodore was Easterman's. But she would want to know whose car it was, and what he was doing in it.

He watched Pete and Andrea enter the store, about to tell Giddy of his offer of part-time work which the store could not afford. Harley held up his hand to indicate he would be five more minutes, and pulled back into the traffic. He turned by the tea rooms. Bryan Gill was standing in the doorway shielding his eyes and gazing up the road for the bus. In the window his wife straightened up the table-cloths, making small last-minute adjustments. Harley was wondering what Easterman would say to him, whether there would be a story, and this time if he would want to hear it.

The traffic is backed as far as I can see. One shiny car top after another. Now and then an opportunist darts into a gap. *Youth*. We say it with a sad shake of the head, a roll of the eyes. The predicted wind has failed to arrive. The hills. The riffs of quiet cloud. We are all waiting. It is hot so everyone has their windows down. Everyone is tuned to a different radio station. In the midst of the rock-station hysteria comes a violin, delicate, insistent. Gunfire and bomb explosions burst from a news bulletin. Now some canned laughter: *Hey, I'm just an ordinary guy. No, really*. There are jingles for ads. It is hard to tell them apart from the pop jingles, which is what advertisers like, of course, as well as, presumably, the US State Department, which has just admitted to a policy of disseminating false information, spraying it out there like weed killer to burn off trails to the truth or maybe flush out a mad man, an assassin, a hijacker. The noises of the world are no longer reliable.

The driver of the van in front of me gets out to try to see where the hold-up is. He stands on the toes of his work boots. His shoulders drop and he turns, looking pissed off, in my direction. He is definitely on the wrong side of glamour—long hair, whiskered growth, a rock star's mo, faded blue overalls. I imagine he got stuck somewhere along the line. I watch him dig around in the back of his van, then he turns and, finding my face in the windscreen, he holds up a beer can and points to it. Shall I? I can't decide. Shall I? Shall I? Looks like I will. I get out of the car. Turns out his name is Frank. He's a furniture polisher. The beer has been in the back of the van a bit long, but hey, this is better than frying in a line of cars that aren't going anywhere. While we stand there drinking, the driver behind me gets out of his car and walks sweatily towards us. He wants to know if he can borrow a mobile. His battery is out. He's late for a meeting and needs to send word. I give him mine. He turns away but we can hear him clearly. He very definitely sounds middle-management. The way he talks up the problem. For the benefit of the other motorists there's a bit of posturing. His gestures are unequivocal. He cuts the air with his hand. He signs off with a Latin thrust of hand-in-the-air. He hands me back the mobile, and without any hesitation at all accepts a can of beer from Frank. What a day, he says. 'Crazy,' he says. 'Absolutely crazy.' His name is Graham—office systems. He says what that is but neither Frank nor I follow up with a question. We sip our beer and watch the traffic shuffle up one place in the outside lane.

Soon—well, we are onto our second beers by this time—a banged-up Subaru nudges forward. We raise our beer cans above our leery faces but our buffoonery barely registers with the man. His hands are stuck to the steering wheel as though he might be going somewhere. I don't know why he can't just abandon ship and slip out for one of Frank's beers. We are all giving him jeering looks when his body slumps forward. Frank looks at me, and strokes his moustache. Graham calls out to him, 'Hey fella. Oi.' He taps on the passenger-side window. Nothing. He opens the door and leans in. Then he stands up and quietly closes the door after him. We watch him straighten a tie, watch him draw a deep breath. He says, 'We have a dead man here.'

The traffic in our lane shuffles forward. The traffic banked up behind has just seen that fresh land opening up in front of Frank's van and they start honking their horns.

So what we do is this. We push the dead man's car to the side of the road in front of Frank's van. I jump in my car and follow Frank up onto the shoulder. Graham parks behind me. We get out of our vehicles. Horns are blaring at us, at the dead man's car holding things up. I try to copy Graham's look of complete indifference. I notice Frank attempting the same. Neither of us are as convincing as Graham. He appears to be genuinely unmoved by the horn-blowing. We wonder what we should do next; there are obvious options and responsibilities, such as phoning the police or an ambulance, but is there any point just yet while the traffic is banked up? We can't leave the dead man there on his own. So we pile into the banged-up Subaru. Frank sits in the front with the dead man. I sit in the back with Graham, all stomach and short knees. We talk about what to do. There's not a lot we can do. We are stuck. Frank has a sound point though. We should try to find out the man's name. Now Graham mutters negatively about tampering with dead bodies. Frank turns around to see what I think of that. Actually, I don't have a problem. We're not going to rob the man. We just need to know who he is. Then what happens is this: the man's mobile phone rings. It's on his person—possibly in the jacket pocket. Frank lets it ring. He waits for the sound of a voicemail message, then he plunges his hand into the dead man's pocket. He's clearly over the consultative thing. He retrieves the message and holds the phone up for me and Graham to listen to a woman who is obviously pissed off. 'I waited for you by the gate. I can't wait any longer. Katie's show begins in ten minutes. I can see her and the other kids looking around for me. In case you've forgotten we're at the park entrance.' In a more facetious voice she names the park, reminds the dead man, Joe (we have a name at last), what city this is, the country and hemisphere, and what time he is expected. 'Just where the hell are you, Joe?' According to the time on the dash he is ten minutes late.

Well, a few minutes later the traffic begins to move. We move Joe into the passenger side of the back seat. Along the way there are some funny looks from passing motorists. Joe doesn't look too good. I've leant him against the door in the back, his head against the window. He's not a good colour. He looks mildly angered by something, perhaps slow service in a restaurant, something of that order. Graham and me park our cars on the shoulder behind Frank's van, then we cram back into Joe's car and continue on into town.

Frank drives, mindful of the speed limit. We find the park. There's the gated entrance the woman spoke of; we drive to the circular green at the end. There's some sort of nativity play happening down in the dell. Kids with cardboard swords, in costume, a gold crown here and there. The parents are standing around in a semi-circle. The women are talking to each other behind their hands. One or two of the men are nearly falling over with boredom.

I'm last out of the car. I make sure I bang the door shut, and a woman—in a light summery cotton dress, a bob of dark hair—turns and looks in our direction, at first without much interest, perhaps just to see where the noise came from. But now we see the mystery catch in her face. She knows that car. She doesn't know us, of course. The questions line up to be answered. Who are these strange men driving up to her daughter's nativity play in Joe's car? Who are we? Why are we here? And where is her husband? Where is Joe? This is the moment Frank steps away from the back window.

the waiting room

She watched television at odd times of the day then complained that she felt 'caught out' if I happened to pop home early. She slept late. We argued over silly things. I knew what was the matter. And she did, too. We were travelling north, that time, into bright clear skies. It was late January and a drought on the east coast of the island had split the hills open. The slightest breeze gave rise to a dust cloud, and where we pitched our tent you could smell the earth on the caked Manawatu riverbed. I thought the great outdoors might turn things around for her and, I suppose, us. We read and spent a lot of time walking the dry river-bed. I had walked ahead this particular afternoon, imagining divorce, a new life, a new woman perhaps, and a new house, street, suburb. Suddenly I remembered Kath. I turned around and found her crouched over, parting driftwood and dry reed, clearing the way either side of a massive claw-mark in the mud.

The next day scientists from the National Museum's Natural History Unit cut out the block of mud with the footprint of *Dinornis robustus*. Television arrived and interviewed Kath on-site. The rest of the holiday was spent combing the riverbed for more footprints.

Home again, and Kath received an invitation from the Natural History Unit to inspect her *Dinornis* footprint. That night she brought home a book on moa. One of its more surprising photographic plates featured the great British anatomist Sir Richard Owen standing next to the skeleton of the towering bird he named *Dinornis novaezelandiae* (prodigious or surprising bird).

For a number of years a copy of this photograph—of the skeleton from Tiger Hill in Otago and the anatomist in his rumpled academic robe—has sat on the mantelpiece next to the photograph of Kath and me whitewater-rafting.

As far as a skeleton is able to, the moa impresses as a rather benign creature. I think it has to do with the kindly tilt of its head in contrast to Sir Richard's grumpiness. Furthermore I suspect the photographer has asked Sir Richard to place his hand on the hip of the *Dinornis*. Probably it is the professor's first contact with a photographer. His mouth shows a wry amusement at the unaccustomed bullying. His left hand is placed familiarly as I mentioned before; and the photographer has achieved something disturbingly conjugal. I can think of no better word than 'gratitude' to describe the slight tilt of the moa's head.

The photograph of the skeleton and the anatomist was the first thing I packed away for this trip.

Then, as the ferry nosed out the heads to the strait, I took out the photograph. The white peaks of the Southern Alps rose above the approaching landfall and, as I looked from one to the other, the *Dinornis* and the view seemed to be clues from two different worlds.

I struck up a conversation with a young blonde woman. A large Canadian flag was sewn onto her backpack. She said she was headed for the lakes. She had flown into Auckland two days earlier. She hoped to be out of here by the end of the week. Queensland beckoned. She had been writing on the back of a postcard while the ferry, newly painted in Mediterranean-white, glided over still blue seas. Whenever the opportunity arose I stole glances at her tanned legs. In June they were like out-of-season fruit.

She asked if I was headed for home. No? You're travelling too—hey, and she groped towards the awkward business of asking whether I was travelling by car. The Subaru was in the garage at home. We intended to walk. I signalled to Kath through the salted windows of the saloon. She was bent over her maps, contemplating the red arrows showing the moa's southern path to extinction. Kath's masters paper described the locomotive speeds of various moa. An excerpt had even made the *Royal Society Journal*.

The Canadian swallowed her disappointment and smiled politely. Kath had come out on deck and so I joined her by the rail. The sun appeared and people carrying their beer glasses began to line the deck. Kath smiled at the approaching landfall. She took my hand in her own, and I set to worrying about the high hopes she had for this trip. The last I saw of the Canadian was coming off the gangway. I happened to look up and catch a shock of blonde hair in the passenger's side of a red sports car.

Half an hour later the Blenheim bus dropped us off at the railway crossing at Tuamarina. A man in the cheese factory said it would be quicker if we continued along the highway another two miles. The way we were headed was longer, less traffic, less chance of a lift, but we liked the sound of Blind Creek Road.

We arrived at the coast in an hour and a half, and walked the next four days.

The coastline, as we began to discover, was a bit of a tease. One point was succeeded by the next one, and we never stopped wondering what lay around that point which of course was just another point, and so on and so on. Meanwhile there were things to look at and examine. Here is a dead seagull. A dead seal. A blue plastic Skeggs fish crate washed ashore. A broken toilet seat. A whiskey bottle. A gin bottle. These bits and pieces stuck with me rather avidly. The same with the erosion north of the Awatere River that has left farm fences suspended over gulches like trapeze wire; the massive shingle platforms of former high tide boundaries; the doorless outhouse tied to the earth in the manner of a tepee. Everything seems so relevant at the start of a journey.

The White Bluffs we had seen from the ferry were suddenly above us. The sun went behind a cloud and we ran laughing beneath the soft, grey papa cliffs to beat the incoming tide. We ran on until we reached the next point—and rounding it, we saw Cape Campbell. It seemed a great distance off, and the intervening coastline looked to have been dealt to with a meat cleaver. On our map the distance from White Bluffs to Cape Campbell was no more than half an inch, but it wasn't until the following afternoon that we reached the lighthouse.

A white picket fence surrounded the grave of a baby girl born late last century. Further along were derelict beaches. We climbed the wooden steps to the lighthouse and the paint came off the rail in our hands. The wind howled off the point, and we sheltered in the lee of the lighthouse, gazing south to that afternoon's walk.

Kath sat on the cold concrete, staring out at the strait. Last night we had had sex. We had been storing up for Kaikoura, when Kath would be at her most fertile. But the previous night we had stayed in an old farmhouse with fires blazing in three rooms. It was full of pastoral art—sheepdog and shepherd sculptures, and winter mustering scenes on the walls. The parents had lost a child to leukaemia, but their religiosity retained a kindly humour. 'God loves mothers' was pinned next to a Steinlager poster of the All Blacks leaping high in the air. Kath and the mother got on fine. She helped in the kitchen with the soup. Every so often she looked up to see how I was getting on with the ten-year-old boy, and rewarded me with warm smiles. These moments convince her that I would be a good father.

'Ray,' she said, as we were packing up to leave the lighthouse. 'Did you see the Chambers' toddler this morning put the toy telephone to the cat's ear?' Kath had looked on with a kind of rapture—transfixed at the spyhole to this other world we can't quite break into. I noticed, as well, the mother watching Kath with her own quiet thoughts.

'Ray,' she said, 'I also had this dream . . .' She shot me a glance to test the air. 'But that I won't tell.'

Kath's stride was full of skip and bounce. The last two days she had walked with her nose to the ground. Now we happily made our way along the lighthouse road, headed south to keep the appointment in Kaikoura. But for the road it would have been slow going. Every so often the wind, which was at our backs, swept out of a divot in the hills and hit us face-on. It was a bruising and tiring day.

Early evening on the fourth day, Kaikoura showed in the distance all fuzzy and warm. Tired, we pushed on. We had left the beach for the road. The offer of a lift would answer a prayer but neither of us dared to hold out a thumb.

Kath gave me a chocolate.

'You know,' she said, 'my feet are blistered. My hair roots are annoying the hell out of me. There's chafing on my inner thigh. Yet, you know what? I'm happy. I feel really good.'

She took my hand and gave it a squeeze.

'So,' she said, further on. 'What's on your mind?'

She tugged my hand.

'Ray?'

'I just hope you're not pegging too much on tonight, that's all. Nothing, really.'

'Well—not really nothing at all. And for that matter I wasn't even thinking . . .'

'All right. All right. My mistake. Let's try a song. Come on. "These boots are made for walking . . ."'

'No,' she said, and just like that the song died in me.

'Steak,' she said a few minutes later. 'I want to eat a steak.'

At some point we stopped for her to pee. A truck soared past. A carousel of light and hissing tyres. Then after, in the perfect silence, came the delicate Japanese sound of Kath's pee. Funny the things you remember.

It was dark so we didn't notice the cloud change until, on the outskirts of Kaikoura, it began to rain. First the wind fell away. It was quiet and we could hear a television set through the trees. Then large cold drops began to fall.

A motorist stopped to look at us, and drove on. We kept to the road alongside the beach. The rain fell on the iron roofs of the cottages. There was a squall from the sea, and the iron roofs gave warning. A few minutes later cold rain struck us face-on. Kath had fallen behind. She made no effort to shield herself; she dragged her blistered heels, and held up her face to the beating. The light from a streetlamp fell across her flushed cheeks. Furious and silent, she limped past me.

I walked ahead again, and half an hour later, from the doorway of the Blue Pacific Hotel bottle store, I watched Kath limp along the esplanade underneath the swaying Norfolk pines. The sea crashed ashore, and the rain hosed down. Halfway across the road to the Blue Pacific she made no attempt to hurry ... Finally, finally, she stepped up onto the footpath, still downcast, and plopped her head against my shoulder.

'I'm sick of this,' she said. 'I just want to be pregnant. I want to be pregnant and stay home and read books.'

In a tiny room at the end of a cavernous hall, Kath shook off her wet clothes. She sat on the bed and kicked her feet loose of the panties. Then she dug around in her knapsack for the pill bottles, and poured a small amount of white powder onto a sheet of notepaper, and this she funnelled into a small single shotglass. She ran the hot-water tap until it was warm and mixed a small amount with the powder. The baking soda solution was supposed to thin out her secretions, or, if you like, put a bit of whip into the flagging tails of the sperm she suspected of being slow finishers.

She lay back on the single bed. Her head fell to one side of the pillow and, while she administered the potion between the legs, she stared at the wallpaper inches away with patient eyes. I wondered if she was thinking of the Chambers' kid. Kath's feet were red and swollen. Chafing had turned her inner thigh raw. For the moment these wounds went unnoticed; with a curious detachment she twirled her finger inside herself. Usually she makes these little preparations elsewhere. Her fine concentration in this regard was a surprise. Outside our window we could hear footsteps in the puddles, beer crates sliding off the back of a truck. Muffled bar talk drifted up through the floorboards and marbled carpet.

Kath turned her head back from the wall.

'Okay, Ray,' she whispered.

She reached up, and we began this act which, like physical therapy, is preoccupied not with what is before us, but with what hopefully will result. Hope, yes. Passion? Well, there has to be, doesn't there? But in this case file it away under polite laughter.

She reached under me to empty the sacs.

Outside the rain had returned with a grudge. It poured, and for a while we lay there listening to it gurgle down the pipes by the window.

'I don't think I'll have that steak now,' she said.

'Why don't you try to bring something in? I don't want to walk another step.' She reached for her watch as she raised her feet onto the bed end. For half an hour Kath was supposed to lie there with her feet up to help everything find its way inside. Waste not, want not. We have pretty well exhausted the jokes.

'Two fish. Or if you can't get that, Chinese. Otherwise a cheeseburger. No onion though. Okay, Ray? I don't think that's unreasonable. This room is too small for onion.'

I woke early next morning. It was so still outside. I left Kath asleep and crept down the hall. Apparently we were the only guests. The doors were all open. At the end, in the window of the bedroom fronting the esplanade, the stars were out in a milky cluster, and, behind the town, like something that had crept up in the night, stood these mountains completely covered in snow.

By mid-morning the sun had caught up to the peaks.

Kath stayed in bed. She said she wanted to give her chafing a chance to heal.

So I went out for a walk. Fresh kelp was piled high on the beach from last night's storm. I could smell it from where I sat in the Garden of Memories at the foot of the memorial to Kaikoura's war dead.

A brackish creek emptied out at the foot of the

gardens. An elderly man in a grey coat took my glance as a sign of interest. 'That's Lyell Creek,' he said, and cleared his throat. 'An eighteen hundred and seventy-nine Road Board decision called for the release of one hundred black swans on Lyell Creek, and the paid employment of a gondola.' This fluency left the man a little breathless, and even embarrassed, as if he had been struck by something outside his control, like hiccups.

Nothing, however, seemed to agree with the warmth of the winter sun—neither the cold peaks, nor the tidy hoovering action of the tide up the bank of loose shingle.

A large bone from the fin of a whale had been casually placed in a bed of polyanthus. At regular intervals tall and curved whale ribs touched points over the path winding through the garden. An information sheet from the visitor centre told their story. The very first inshore whalers had caught the pups and led the mothers inshore to be slaughtered. In no time at all the inshore waters were cleaned out. First the whales, then their predators drifted away. The whalers left behind a few oil pots and shipwreck timber, an enormous quantity of bones and a residual carelessness that is to be found just about everywhere. In the Garden of Memories the bones had recently been spray-painted and the surrounding leaves of karaka trees had copped a white dusting. Same with the grass at the foot of each whale rib; it had been needlessly and sloppily sprayed.

Kath was still in bed—captive and listless. She lay there looking at her fingernails. I'd opened the door too suddenly and given her quite a start, which, in turn, quickly passed to resentment—the old look of the bad old days.

Once outside, though, her spirits lifted. It was warmer in the noon sun than inside the Blue Pacific. We followed the curve of the beach for the Pier Hotel, bathed in sunshine, on the point where the fishing boats were moored.

We asked for and got the room with the sun porch facing the sea.

Mrs Fender said we would be sharing dinner with the hotel trustees that evening.

When we entered the dining room a plump man in a brown suit called out the seating arrangements: 'Boy, girl. Boy, girl . . .' Nearly all the trustees were elderly, and a feisty chap with broken blood vessels in his face made a big show of Kath sitting next to him.

A waitress brought two carafes to each table. She went to pour Kath's glass, but Kath placed her hand over it.

'Give her some red then,' said the man with broken blood vessels.

'Kerry,' the man's wife said firmly.

Once again Kath politely declined the wine, and the woman, with the quiet glee of having solved a riddle, clapped her hands.

'You're with baby, dear?'

Kath blushed; then, to my surprise, she nodded.

'Oh wonderful,' the woman said.

Kath glanced away from me. She looked happy. The woman asked the baby's date of arrival, and how long she planned to stay in hospital, and would she breast-feed, and without missing a beat Kath provided answers. She said she planned to stay at home. But only for a short while. 'Yes,' the woman said guardedly. She was quite a bit older. Five grandchildren. But Kath's knowledgable talk of creches, and a plan—which we had never discussed before—to get a nanny on board as soon as possible drew a questioning look from the woman. She didn't say anything however. Perhaps that would come out later on the drive home with her husband.

We finished dinner and on the way up the stairs Kath said, 'Not a word please, Ray.'

The week passed slowly at the Pier Hotel. Each morning Kath took her temperature. It remained steady, without the telltale variation she hoped for. Kath said it wasn't important. Such tests are at best an indication, but hardly scientific. We went out for walks. We just strolled about, nothing too strenuous. On the beach I noticed she stepped warily. Of course I kept getting ahead of her. Once I happened to glance up to the coast road and I thought I saw a red sports car on the sun-lit bends. I looked harder. I decided I must have imagined it. 'What?' she asked when I walked back to where she stood in the shingle. Her hand was circling her belly. It was as if she was willing something to happen.

We visited the library. We sat in there with the pensioners and terminally unemployed. We read the newspapers. Up north a Maori radical delighted in a demographic trend promising Maori would out-number Pakeha by the year 2050. In *Doonesbury*, AIDS-infected Andy was going out of this world with great style. It was hard to believe that his creator would really let him go. But on our second-to-last morning in Kaikoura, I brought the *Press* upstairs, and said to Kath, 'Andy's dead.'

Finally, Kath's blisters had healed. The chafing had disappeared.

We left at first light, and walked along Avoca Road to the point. In the half-light we wandered past the

Fyffe homestead with its house piles made of whale-bone vertebrae. We might have stopped for another reason: in the late eighteen-fifties, with the digging of the house foundations, a moa egg the size of six hen's eggs was discovered. A few days earlier I had visited and found the house addition to be part of a ship's cabin. The resident curator said its pink paint was made from whalebone oil. A stack of rib bones stood in a corner with a yard broom. A toilet seat was covered with two ancient strips of sheepskin. In the window hung a tea towel of a fox hunt.

We stopped outside a small bach with a shingle that read, 'Beware of the dog, Kung Fu' and a few other filthy Japanese words.

'My god,' she said. 'Tell me that isn't a moa neck and head.'

Mounted on an old tree stump was a length of curved punga. I couldn't quite see what she was getting at. I didn't say anything of course.

We took the cliff-top route to South Bay and, where the road joined up with the main road south, we stopped for tea and gingernuts. At our feet, lying in the roadside grass, was an aluminium capsule of Berocca effervescent vitamin B tablets with a .22 bullet-hole in its side—that raised a laugh.

For the rest of the day we tramped south. At the

Kahutara river mouth the road linked up with the beach and we walked high above the rocks where the seals lolled in beds of kelp.

The sun left the road early afternoon and the rest of the way we walked in the shade of the hill and on a black road.

'Ray,' Kath said. 'What do you think of the name "Humphrey"? I told that woman at the Pier we were calling our baby Humphrey, but I've just realised, wasn't there a famous sea elephant or something called Humphrey? I mean, personally, I don't mind. But I thought you might.'

'I don't,' I said, and that was as much as we said for the next hour.

I settled into a rhythm, and daydreamed about nothing in particular. I can't say what actually pulled me out of it. An instinct, edgy and expectant I suspect, rather than Kath's shouting. I turned in time to see Kath sit down on the roadside. She just sat down and put her head between her knees. A car hissed past. Strange faces lined the windows. She kept her head hanging there. She said, 'It's come . . . My baby . . . Oh god, Ray. Look at me.'

We stayed in Oaro that night, at the guesthouse of another farmer retired from the hill country. The one before had had arthritis in his ankles. This one had artificial hips. He was very attentive, and concerned for Kath as she wouldn't leave the bedroom.

He said, 'We can keep her dinner for her. Maybe she needs some aspirin.'

Her insomnia kept me awake and I spent the whole night on my side unable to face her. In the morning she said she wanted to go home.

'I said, I want to go home.'

'Right. I heard you the first time.'

'The last thing I want is another day of this,' she said, pulling on her boots.

'Follow the railway lines. You'll be right,' the farmer said. 'The tide's high though. I don't know what you'll do past Mikonui.'

At Oaro the road swung inland for Christchurch, and we did as the farmer advised and followed the railway tracks alongside the coast.

I don't know why we can't have kids. There is no clinical reason, at least none that we haven't already explored. The journey—and this place where we had arrived—were all too familiar.

In the distance we could make out the aptly named Spy Glass Rock—a neat oval on the far point. Short of there, the inshore water looked to have made its peace with the bluffs. The water there looked deep and settled. The likely way around the point was over the bluff, or we could take the railway tunnel ahead.

'So,' I said. 'What's your preference, Kath?'

She said she didn't care.

'Course you care.'

'Either or . . . You decide. I don't care.'

'You should care.'

'No, Ray. I don't. I don't feel anything. I could climb Everest right now. Anyway, I don't see why I should decide.'

'Fine,' I said. Although my mind wasn't made up until we were almost upon the tunnel, and without another word I dropped down to the beach and found us two sticks.

The tunnel entrance was dark and rather threatening. Whenever we have ventured this close to a tunnel or cave, we have gotten a bad case of the heebie-jeebies. Not a word this time. There was no encouraging pinpoint of light to aim for, which I took to mean that the tunnel, somewhere along the line, curved.

We walked along the rubble between the railway track and the tunnel wall. In no time it was dark and very cold. The sound of the sea washing ashore was replaced by the raspy noise of our stick ends tracing the tunnel wall. It was the only way of going forward. Otherwise the tunnel was black and directionless.

We walked for maybe ten minutes before a word was spoken.

'This is stupid, Ray. Stupid.'

'It's also faster.'

'What if a train comes?'

'We lie down,' I said. There was ample room between the tracks and the tunnel wall.

'I don't like this. I want you to know that,' she said.

And a few minutes later, 'You always have to go that bit further, don't you? Never mind that it means risking all. Or anybody else.'

There was a chirping sound overhead, and the sudden beating of small wings. It might have been bats. But, had Kath asked for my opinion, I would have said I thought the noise belonged to birds.

After a moment, she said, 'Ray?'

'Yep?'

'Are you scared?'

'Yes,' I said.

'Then walk faster. I do not like it in here one little bit.' Her hand touched my shoulder with a slight shove. 'Go,' she said impatiently. She got round me okay. We must have reached the start of the bend because the light in the tunnel entrance had squeezed to a pale quarter moon.

Small rocks turned over as Kath charged on ahead.

Once she stopped and called back, 'Ray, are you still there?'

'Still here,' I said.

A moment later I heard her cry out. 'Jesus. Ray, I've dropped my stick.'

She was on all fours. I couldn't see her of course. But I could hear the light scuffing sound of her hands feeling around the loose rocks for her dropped stick.

I called ahead of me, into that darkness. 'Okay. Don't move. Just stay where you are. I'm coming, Kath. Keep talking to me.'

At the same time I began to wonder, what if a train was to come through now? It was a stupid time to wonder what we were doing here, and how it was we had arrived here at all. It was kind of a stupid moment to realise you did actually care for somebody else after all.

'Kath,' I said, pushing her name ahead of me.

'I'm here, Ray.'

Thank god. She was ten metres or so ahead.

'Kath. Make sure you are against the tunnel wall.'

'I am, Ray. I'm kneeling on the side of the track, I think.'

I told her to keep calling to me. Finally, a voice almost underneath me called up, 'I'm here, Ray.' Her hands touched my knees. My thigh. My jacket. She climbed up me like this, until she had regained her feet.

'Hold my hand, Kath.' She took hold of my left hand. My right hand held the stick. It was pitch-black; the only sound was the stick end dragging against the wall.

'I shouldn't have rushed. I'm sorry, Ray.'

'Shush,' I said. 'Listen.'

We could hear the sound of the stick against the wall. Behind us it was impossible to see, and so it was ahead, too, but I felt we must be at the curve, now, and that soon we would have something to aim for.

She wasn't talking to him, and he wasn't talking to her. It was over the dog again. Their own dog, Elgar, and the mutt across the road. Elgar and the dog in question were always sniffing each other's butts. She was worried about the consequences. She thought Elgar and the other dog were totally unsuited to each other. Elgar was short, built low to the ground, a tail-wagger. The dog across the road stood on spindly legs and was known to be a depressive. His wife had gone on at length; at first it had been amusing, but then she got so over-the-top she wouldn't let it alone, and so he had begged to differ. He had put it to her that breeding followed its own logic, that the laws of nature sorted everything out in the end. Why get wound up over nothing? The word 'nothing' seemed to have done it. She rounded on his laziness, his come-what-may attitude to everything in life. He dared to ask if she was premenstrual, and things went from bad to worse.

The dog looked miserable. It sat on its mat in the kitchen looking up at the two of them. It looked so sorry to have caused all this. For that matter, even the trees out the window looked sorry.

She had a way of making anger rise from her shoulders. Right now her shoulders were furious as she stood with her back to him, working at the bench. His own hands were deep in his pockets. Something needed to be said. Definitely something needed to be said. This was silly. He thought, I should really say something. I really should. And then: Why is it always me? Why was it always up to him to make the situation better? Besides, he could see how it would end up. It was boring even to think about. He would offer to talk to the neighbours about their dog. Then he would apologise for picking up the ball after she had told the dog in no uncertain terms that it was to leave the ball alone. The ball only got the dog excited. It would run around inside the house and in its excitement fart a lot. And they were expecting guests, and she didn't want to see their faces suddenly tighten up and the tips of their prissy little noses dance around the odour in the hall where the dog had leapt farting in the air for the ball. So he would say he was sorry. Then what? She would sigh and lean her head back against his chest and she would say she was sorry too—she probably shouldn't have used that tone. She knew he meant well. He loved the dog. The problem would turn out to be not the dog, but some shitty office stuff she'd brought home from work.

What he said in the end was that he would take the dog out for a walk. The time wasn't right, he knew that: the guests were due to arrive any minute. But that was half the point: he didn't care. Normally it would have provoked a cry of disbelief from his wife. 'What do you mean? Joe and Cass are due here any minute. They're bringing a house guest, someone or other. What do you mean . . .?' But instead she said, 'Go,' because to maintain her staunch silence was marginally more satisfying than to remind him of his responsibility. 'To our guests,' she might have added. But she had said 'go' like she didn't care if he was there or not. She didn't even turn around. She snatched at the vegetable knife. As he backed out the front door with the dog on the lead he could hear the knife on the chopping board. Boy, was she pissed off. Good, he thought. He nodded down at the pavement. Good. Fuck her. Good—again, nodding at the house, and now inhaling the cool night. It felt good. It felt fantastically good.

The dog looked up at him with its moist, trusting eyes and he felt a surge of love for it. Well, he wasn't missing anything, really, was he? The dog opened its mouth to release its tongue out the side of its gummy jaw. Sometimes a dog knew exactly what you were thinking. The dog dropped its eyes. It sniffed at the road ahead. It wagged its tail and walked with a skip in its step. He thought, I love this dog. (And: I have never really shown it enough love, the love that I really actually feel.)

His wife would be aerosoling the hallway and swinging the front door back and forth to let in the night air. Any minute now the guests would roll up. This was the time to turn around; if he did he'd probably make it back in time. But look at what was happening: he was walking in the other direction. There is, he thought, a certain momentum to following a dog with a wagging tail. He could imagine the scene at home. The guests in the lounge, exchanging glances and whispers. From the kitchen the false cheer of Gina's voice. That in itself would be enough for the guests to put two and two together. Gina would roll in with a plate of filo pastries. Probably it would be as she lowered the plate onto the coffee table that she would let it out that they'd had a fight. 'Bill's got the pip. He's gone off into the night somewhere . . .' And that would be that. The funny thing is, having imagined this little scene, it was like it had already happened, and now there was no point in turning back. The only problem was staying out until the guests left.

It was cold—not too cold but cold enough that if he stopped walking the air would seep through his clothing and attack his bones.

They were by the edge of a small park. Elgar sometimes liked to crap on the grass there. Elgar stopped and raised his snout. He moved around on his short legs and stared intelligently into the dark, from which direction came a low growl. And Elgar leapt. The stupid mutt forgot he was on a lead. He seemed to fly forwards and backwards at the same time. Mid-air he wore a disgruntled look, a look of canine annoyance.

The other dog emerged from the shadows, walking around and sniffing the grass the way dogs do right before they lift a leg. It was a small, shaggy-haired Great Dane, if there is such a thing. One of those haphazardly crossed dogs Gina was worried about Elgar fathering.

Now he was aware of someone else there, at the edge of the dark, sitting on the bench.

A woman's voice said, 'Hello.'

'Hi,' he said back, and he was of half a mind to apologise because at night the world was a different place. People preferred to lay down some distance between themselves. The park was small to begin with. If it wasn't for Elgar the woman would have cause for concern; she would have seen a man straying into her territory without reason. She probably would have stood up and called her dog to her.

Instead she called Elgar to her and Elgar walked happily over. He sniffed her feet, her legs. The woman didn't seem to mind. In fact, she laughed. She even allowed Elgar to lick her hands. She didn't sound scared at all; if anything she was actually quite friendly. She asked about Elgar's breed.

'Elgar is a Jack Russell,' he told her.

'Elgar.' The way she had said Elgar—it was with an accent. Even Elgar stopped what he was doing to look up at the woman. She gave a fluttery wave. 'Hello, Elgar. How do you do?' she said. Elgar stared back at her with his tongue hanging out the side of his mouth. He was expecting food of course.

'That's a nice name. My dog, it is called Jess.' The other dog looked up at hearing its name. It looked at the woman, and now at Bill. While Bill thought about what he could say next, the dog stared through him as if, Bill thought, it had just comprehended the moment at hand and seen right through it.

The woman moved to make space for him on the bench, and Bill made a shivery noise as he sat down.

Well, it was cold—that much was true. It was that slow, seeping cold. He stuck his hands in his pockets for warmth. The woman wore a ski jacket with a hood. She wriggled closer. He could feel the bulk of the ski jacket. He could feel the cold of the slats pushing up through his thin trousers. For the moment they watched the dogs. Elgar was sniffing Jess's butt. Jess's patient snout and Elgar's wagging tail—it was as if they were the one dog. He had a terrible feeling about what was going to happen next; he knew Elgar's moves. The scratching of his front paws. The darting excitement which now, sure enough, resulted in the appearance of his little pink dog prick. Jess moved away and Elgar skittishly caught up and placed his paws on Jess's back.

The woman laughed. She raised her knee and crossed her legs. Now Jess rolled over onto her back. She dropped her front paws and looked over at the two strangers seated on the bench. Elgar looked as well. His ears pricked, his tail still wagging madly.

The woman said, 'I like your dog. He's cute. Aren't you, Elgar?' Elgar grinned back.

Bill thought he should probably get up from the bench and drag Elgar off. His little prick was showing eagerness. A year ago, after he'd pulled Elgar off a dog tied up to a bike-stand outside a dairy, Elgar had snapped his jaws on his wrist. 'Come here, Elgar,' he said now, and clicked his fingers. Besides, he was cold. It was too cold to sit around at this hour of night. He needed to get moving. It was still too early to go back to the house. The guests would have only just sat down to the main.

He was about to get up when the woman said it was unusual to see anyone out. She said she had brought the dog here at night all week and this was the first time she'd encountered another soul. This time he caught her accent. Polish, she said, when he asked. When she said Polish it had felt like an invitation to look deeper into her face, to perhaps ascertain a Polish look. Her skin was very pale but in a luminous way. Her eyes were bright. He tried to think what he knew of Poland. Gdansk. The name filtered up from the television news of a decade ago, men with moustaches, gathering in mist, fists raised. 'Poland, really? And whereabouts in Poland?' he asked. She replied with an unpronounceable name—somewhere he'd never heard of. He really didn't know that much about Poland. He was on the brink of mentioning Zátopek but worried that he had that wrong, that the runner was Finnish, or maybe even Hungarian. It was a muddled part of the world. So he asked her the inevitable question: What she was doing here in this part of the world? In a park with a dog named Jess? She couldn't have brought Jess from Poland. Once upon a time film actresses did that sort of thing, but no one who was serious in the world did that sort of thing anymore.

She said Jess belonged to the kind people she was staying with. She said she was here for a conference. What kind of conference? She smiled into the dark. This time he noticed her mouth, her lips more full than he had appreciated. Well, it was a special kind of conference. It was a conference for the physically disabled. Really? She didn't look disabled. Maybe she was a spokesperson, maybe an academic? No, she said. She was disabled. As she said this she smiled and nodded at the ground. He could tell she was pleased at his surprise.

'Really?' he said, because it really was that kind of surprise. And in spite of himself, he couldn't help making a quick inspection of her body and limbs. The woman didn't notice or care. She was looking over at the dogs. Elgar was licking Jess's private parts. Bill felt a heave in his gut. He was on the brink of calling Elgar off the other dog. First, he turned his head—he had the impression the woman wasn't thinking anything like, This is disgusting. He had a good view of her face and nothing Elgar was doing seemed to have changed her opinion of him. She moved her leg next to his. She said, 'Here, you may touch, please.'

Bill laid his hand on her thigh. She was wearing jeans.

'Lower,' she said, picking up his hand and now dropping it below the knee. 'Harder.' He wasn't sure what he was supposed to feel. It just felt like a leg. 'Okay,' she said, 'make a fist please.' She had to close his fingers for him. 'Now knock on leg.' He knocked and Jesus it was as hard as knocking on a door. She told him, 'I lost both legs in a car accident.' She explained what had happened. She wasn't even driving. She was walking across a car park. That's all she remembered—walking across a car park, and then waking up in hospital. Luckily there were witnesses and what they saw went like this. A ten-year-old kid left in the car by his mother jumped into the driver's seat. He was fooling around with the ignition and playing with the gears and the next thing the car reversed at great speed. The car bumper caught the woman just below the knees and pinned her against a wall. The witnesses said the kid had no idea what he had done. He didn't know he'd pinned a woman to the wall. He was just freaking out over the car taking off backwards. The car had gone as far as it could but the kid must have panicked because he kept his foot down on the accelerator, the wheels spinning. Jesus, he thought.

It occurred to him to ask her name.

She told him. She said her name meant 'flower'. He told her it was a beautiful name. He wasn't bullshitting. It was a beautiful name. Both its sound and its meaning. It was the most beautiful name he had ever heard. She laughed. No, really, he insisted. It's beautiful. He had never sounded so sincere.

It was cold, though, and this time when he shivered she made the comment: 'They said it would be spring and so I brought no winter clothes. I had to borrow this jacket. But there is no spring. Here the flowers appear and the trees bud but it is an ice sun.'

She moved closer until their sides pressed together, his leg against her. He said, 'You're right. It is bloody cold here.'

The woman took his hand and blew. She said he could have some of her Polish heat. Laughing, she blew into both hands. It was strangely erotic—ticklish, of course. Bill said he liked her heat, her Polish heat. She laughed at this as if he had told a joke. She said she was pleased to find someone out at night. He was pleased too. As pleased as she was, if not more so. It wasn't every day that he met someone like her—someone from Poland whose name meant 'flower'. In fact she was the first Pole he had ever met.

'You are welcome,' she said, in that foreign way of aping American politeness, which ordinarily was even more grating coming from foreigners.

He rubbed his hands together, even though he wasn't really that cold anymore. Excited, but not really cold.

'You are cold,' she said.

'Just a bit,' he said. And with that she reached her arm behind him and pulled him into her side.

'I am cold. It is so cold here,' she said. 'They said it would be spring . . . I expected warm . . .'

'Are you cold?'

'Yes, I think . . .' She shivered for him. 'Feel.' She placed her face next to his, cheek to cheek. Her face was shiny with cold.

They laughed and as they turned their faces in towards each other they kissed. It took him by surprise but only for a fraction of a moment. He wasn't expecting to kiss her, but now that he was—or they were—it seemed to be the most natural thing in the world. His first Polish kiss. She kissed hungrily, and when they broke away he was pleased to hear her breathe excitedly. She tore at the zipper on her ski jacket. He reached inside to all that warm clothing and found her breast, her Polish breast. He felt her smiling Polish cheek against his own. Once more they turned to kiss.

The next time they broke off—to breathe—Bill noticed the dogs. Elgar's prick was out. Crudely pink and practically trembling with its own little urgency. His own prick was trying to break out of his trousers. The Polish woman whatshername 'flower' had her hand there. Now she took his hand all very daintily and placed it over her crotch.

Here, she told him. Take these things off. He had to stand up to pull off her jeans. Well, he had to take off her shoes. He got those off, peeled off the jeans. He had started on the stockings when she told him not to bother. The stockings came with the lower legs. She told him to take off her legs. He hadn't ever thought about a thing like this before. He imagined they would unscrew at the knees. He didn't want to ask but he thought they probably would come off clockwise, though in Europe these things sometimes worked in reverse, like light switches, and hot- and cold-water taps. Anyway, it wasn't like unscrewing legs off a table. It was nothing like what he expected. The moulded parts fitted over the leg ends like capped teeth. He had to help her with the strappings.

It was much easier than he would have imagined,

had he at any point previously—say while travelling alone in a bus through the night—stopped to think what it would be like to remove a woman's legs. He unstrapped the left leg. He placed it next to the other stump on the bench where he had sat. It was funny how much he knew, how much of it seemed to come naturally to him, this practical side of making love to a legless woman. The logistics—for example picking her up in his arms and seating himself in the same place she had sat, balancing her on his thighs while she undid his belt. He wriggled out of his trousers and underpants and raised her. Clearly she was practised at the rest. It was a great fuck. If anything it was helped by the fact she didn't have those legs. The weight of the Polish woman was more centrally condensed. He had to provide most of the movement but that was okay. She came. Then he came. She slumped forward and over his shoulder. He saw that the dogs were still fucking. Elgar looked up, and he felt embarrassed to have his own dick out in front of Elgar. Elgar calmly dismounted Jess and walked over to sniff some grass and gaze up at the dark treetops. Elgar was in one of his quiet, contemplative moments. An intelligent calm settled between his snout and his eyes. Whereas the Polish woman's dog ran around in small excited circles. Elgar ignored her. He sat patiently, ready to move on.

The Polish woman was slumped against him; she grunted and laughed. She rubbed her nose against his shoulder. He wanted to thank her. Bill wanted to tell her that she had saved his night. But that sounded a little too over the top. He didn't want to scare her. He certainly didn't want her to think he was hopeful of another meeting in the not-too-distant future. That's not how these things happened or were supposed to happen. As he glanced up at the frozen black sky he happened to catch a shooting star on its singular journey. Why not leave it at that? He'd been out with Elgar when he'd spotted another dog. That was all the world needed to officially know. He tried to guess the hour. He pictured his wife at the door. The guests taking their rosy faces out to the car. He would go home and apologise to Gina. He'd had a good long walk with Elgar. Plenty of time to think. And now he would say he was sorry. When he knew guests were on their way he should never have gotten the dog so excited.

broken machinery

It was in my second year of high school that she moved out. The briskness with which I was despatched to McDonald's that Friday night somehow connected with her urgency to get on with a new life. Saturday morning Mum was packed and gone. There had been no serious arguments. No shouting. Late Saturday morning I went back to McDonald's, this time with Dad. We walked there in a daze. There was nobody else involved, at least not then; but had there been, Dad would have had an easier time understanding.

For a while he sniffed at the air, expecting perfume, and where he'd grown used to a familiar voice there came, instead, this new silence. From his rapt concentration on papers strewn over his desktop he tended to look up suddenly, as if touched by a chill that had started at the base of his spine. Then he'd rip his glasses off his face, ready to confront the devil.

'Pete! Jesus,' he said. 'Please don't creep up on me like that.'

I had my mother's old office. It was only now she was gone that we referred to it as my mother's office, and after school I went there to help out with what had been her responsibilities. I rolled the *Tomorrow's Bride* into cardboard cylinders ready to be slipped into letter-boxes. Four times a year the *Bride* crept up one wall of yellow-painted hessian, almost to touch the ceiling. The rest of the time, if there wasn't much doing, I got to answer the telephone.

The last digit on the telephone next to me was different from the one in Dad's office. Late afternoon it would be Mum calling to see how I was making out; we chatted away and through the glass partition I saw Dad frown at his desktop.

Mum said, 'Why don't you start calling me Helen? Would you like that?'

'If you want to,' I said.

'It's not what I want, Pete, honey. It's what you want. That's what's important. If you want to call me Helen, go right ahead.'

After I hung up Dad came through and stood, friendly, his hands deep in his pockets rattling change.

'So, what's your mother's news?'

'Nothing much.'

'Go on,' he said, with a kind of embarrassed grin. 'She must have said something.'

I said, 'She wants me to call her Helen.'

Dad laughed. He chuckled all the way back to his desk. He shook his head at something lodged in his memory.

I was the result of what he called his 'boom' period. I followed on the heels of the Porsche. While I was at primary school we moved from the cramped semi-detached without a view to the two-storey house on the hill. One of the bedrooms Dad took for an office. A desk was pushed hard up beneath the window, which overlooked the valley of motley tin roofs; the view escaped the hills and ran out towards the heads. I think of him in there with the telephone grafted to his ear, kissing Helen's forehead when she brought in his morning tea and cheese crackers. Still on the telephone, he might lift a scrap of paper with doodlings and my mother's eyes would pop. Then she'd nod approvingly at the figures, and rumple his thin, lifeless hair, which belonged more to a fat boy than my father. Then she might kiss his balding spot and rub it as if making a wish. That's what I remember.

But the winter she became Helen Jefferson, instead of chatting about her university classes I wanted to tell her that not everything was as it should be with the *Bride*. My job got easier. The publication got thinner, down to an anaemic thirty pages, with not half the advertising of the old days. I had no complaints. The *Bride* was more easily packaged. Plus we could carry more in the van borrowed from Uncle Dirk, and so it took less time to distribute.

'The market's shot,' was all Dad would say.

'Why?' I asked. Why should a good thing end?

'Why? Why anything . . .' he said. Dad pushed back from his desk on his swivel chair and stared out the window, found a flock of starlings and followed their black shiver against the dusk; a nerve was sprung and the flock suddenly broke west.

'These things can happen without warning. Without so much as a hint of what lies around the corner,' he said. 'I'm not even sure asking "Why?" is the best way of going about it. What can I tell you . . .'

'Mum used to say that,' I said.

'Did she?' he said. What else? he was going to say. Instead he settled for, 'She's smarter than most. I can tell you that.'

He drummed his fingers on the windowsill, trying to re-focus. I see now it was just a matter of getting something in his sights. Not surprisingly, the moment he lifted his attention from the publication, the first thing to catch his eye was destined to become an obsession.

It just happened to be squash. Those short July afternoons, the office routine took a turn with Dad picking me up outside the school gates and driving off to the squash club. He ran about the court like a wounded beast. Crashed off the walls and came back to the receiver's side drenched and glowing unhealthily, his jaw slack. 'Another game,' he gasped, and in this final game I contented myself with bringing the ball back into the centre court, nice and easy.

An idea began to take shape when Dad, discovering that he had lost four kilos, reacted as if he had gained something. Saturday morning we motored into town. In the jeans boutique loud with rock'n'roll Dad grimaced his way inside the doors and, without a word to the thin shop assistant, pointed to what he wanted from the rack and threw down a plastic card on the glass counter. He took to wearing jeans and sweatshirts to the office.

In August, instead of getting out and hustling space for the traditional bumper Christmas issue, we went skiing at Mt Hutt. What gave him that idea? What clues can be found in a person who has never before expressed any interest in skiing?

'What's got into him, Pete?' my mother, Helen Jefferson, wondered during our telephone conversations.

The afternoon we were to leave for the South Island, I came home to find a stranger foraging in the boot of the Porsche. 'Oh, hello, Pete,' he said, and stood straighter than normal, next to our new ski equipment. He looked sour, and this I would say was due to his determination to get over and done with this moment in which I should note, and perhaps comment favourably on, the mass of curly hair, which was a good deal more dark and lively than it had been when he stepped from the shower that morning.

I don't think he cared one way or the other for the skiing. On the chairlift he sat more like a commuter than an enthusiast. We did get friendly with a group of university girls. Most mornings we piled on the bus which took us up the slopes, and with the girls Dad threw back his head and laughed longer and louder than necessary. The girls all called him Graeme. I was happy for him—everything was going sweet. But maybe he pushed himself too far, too soon. Late in the day when he was bone-weary he stumbled coming off the chairlift, ending up sprawled in the snow. His lips were pressed together, and the corrugations in his chin deepened and didn't match up at all well with his perm. It looked as if two different faces had been hurriedly pieced together after an accident.

After that he pottered about at the bottom of the lifts. He waved me onto the chair with the girls and we waved back at this stranded man in sunglasses and mittens standing like a pointsman in the snow. His hands clasped behind his back, he just stood there and watched, and resisted all the vertical motion of the mountain. At night he rubbed moisturiser into his face. His skin darkened. Then it got tighter, to the point where he stayed inside the lodge during the last two days rather than risk another dose of mountain sun pulling it apart.

He was more excited about the homeward trip. On the ferry he kept disappearing to rub moisturiser into his face. Once we were out of the swell he stayed on deck, standing at the rail with the rest of the passengers, staring back at the bulging shorn hills reeling us inside the harbour. Around Pt Jerningham the city surprised, and Dad stepped back from the rail. He spun around, saw the terminal rear into view and checked himself.

'How do I look, Pete?'

'Okay,' I said. 'You've still got your sunglasses on.'

'Right. The sunglasses.' He touched their rim then took his hand away. 'Look all right, do they?'

'Sure.'

'I can always take them off.'

'Whatever you're comfortable with,' I said. 'I just wanted to point them out.'

'Well, thanks, Pete, but I'm finding it a bit glary. How are you finding it . . . Phew,' he said.

'It's definitely in our eyes,' I said, and Dad, shielding his from the imaginary glare, pointed vaguely with his free hand to the gluey haze over Tinakori Hill.

Inside the terminal Helen stood to one side of the exit doors. She knew about our failure to book the car on the ferry. Over the phone she had insisted on picking us up. 'I want to, Pete,' she had said, rather sharply in the end. She saw me now and waved. She had on large rimmed sunglasses so only the corners of her mouth indicated a smile.

'There she is, Dad,' I said, and just like that he dropped six hundred dollars' worth of skis. Like a man racked by sharp chest pains. That's how he later explained it. Other passengers following behind had to jump quickly to either side. Dad kept looking at Helen, but the way he looked it was as if he was combing his memory for something, a code that clearly wasn't there anymore. Helen had taken off her sunglasses and was waving and smiling. I hissed at Dad to whip off his sunglasses. He didn't hear, and it was never clearer: all the old confidence of the household Helen Jefferson had taken with her when she left.

Now she kissed Dad's cheek, then talked a streak as if she'd won something. 'Well ... so, how was it? Absolutely brilliant, I bet. Well, come on, you two. I'm taking you both to Pizza Hut.'

Severely sunburnt, his skin moist, and hanging in there with the sunglasses, Dad hunched up like a circus bear in Helen's small Honda. At Pizza Hut he and Helen sat at opposite ends of the cubicle. I kept my head down in the middle and picked away at a bowl of french fries.

'New jeans, Gray,' she said. 'I did notice.'

Dad blushed and whipped off his sunglasses and where the mountain sun hadn't burnt there were goggle-size white rings around his eyes. My mother burst out laughing. 'Oh Gray, you should see yourself.'

We never went back to the squash club—neither of us mentioned it. Dad grew out his perm and went back to his old slacks and blazer. He kept saying how badly he had fallen behind.

He had great intentions—leaving for the office very early—but by mid-afternoon he was done for.

Overwhelmed, he sat before a desk that no longer seemed right; its top was vast and unconquerable, as if in the time Dad had taken to duck out for the mail the desk had asserted its own autonomy. It started with the desk, but gradually spread to other things that had been an integral part of Dad. I hardly ever saw him on the telephone anymore.

Soon there was no longer any point in dropping by the office, and at home I found him stretched out along the couch, reading, and writing letters to friends whose names I associated with the old household. People who used to come to dinner; others who had since moved away.

He spent hours in the kitchen. It was a new thing for him, as the squash had been and the skiing was intended to be. He always had his face in a cookbook, and during the last term, when I walked in from school, I would be asked to sample something, to sip from the ladle a Chinese soup he'd laboured over that afternoon.

He mentioned the lease on his office ending in November, that he didn't think he would renew it. A few nights later—he had cooked enchiladas and chopped tabouleh—he said he was putting the *Bride* on the market.

'Time to move on to other things . . .' He checked me for a response, then got up from the table.

Trouble was, apparently nobody thought the publication worth moving into. Yet what would have once presented itself as a problem, Dad disregarded. He had his reasons. The house market had changed. First-home owners weren't building anymore, and so the publication, with its advice on how to subcontract and achieve a low-cost new house, was an idea fallen on hard times.

The truth is, Dad allowed the *Bride* to lapse into receivership. The outstanding bills were for small amounts and when I came to understand such things it confounded me why he, why anyone, should have allowed a business with such a solid track record to be shot down by shrapnel. At the time it was less noticeable and, if anything, consistent with how he was managing the rest of his life.

Labour Weekend, a sunny Monday afternoon, we drove around the bays to Days Bay for ice-creams. We mingled with other families by the duck pond. We hired a dinghy and rowed out beyond the wharf. Dad lay back in the bow and opened up his face the way he had on the ski slopes. We didn't talk much but he was able to respond and chuckle at small things—a silver splash as a kahawai broke near the bow to scatter a shoal of herrings and, in the shadows beneath the wharf, the half-panicky delighted yelps from a dinghy-load of girls pursued by a dinghy-load of boys in wet jeans.

It was on the way home that the Porsche's muffler finally dropped onto the road. At Seaview, as well, something that sounded like a box of marbles rolling about made him pull over to the roadside. We got out of the car; Dad kicked the grille and the bonnet leapt up. Then he thought the better of it. The time was past when he might have rolled up his sleeves and set about correcting what had gone wrong. I don't know whether the parts were too far gone or whether he just couldn't be bothered. He removed the house keys from the keyring—the car keys he left on the driver's seat—and without a word we walked the mile to Hutt Park, where Dad called a taxi. I suppose he was doing what was easiest.

We had to borrow Uncle Dirk's van to clear his office. Dad chose to do it at night, which probably had something to do with his feelings as the longest tenant on the ground floor. Back and forth, we carted out back issues of the *Bride*, pens and charts, files; we filled boxes. In a desk drawer he found a passport photo of Helen Jefferson, taken before their trip to Honolulu. The three weeks they were away I stayed with Uncle Dirk.

'Here's your mother,' he said, handing me the photo.

'Best leave the desk and chairs, Pete.' He gave the office a final once-over. 'Come on,' he said. 'What time is your mother expecting you?'

'About now,' I said.

'What? Nine already? Christ's sakes, Pete, why didn't you say?'

We dumped everything in the garage. Boxes and boxes. The bottom of one collapsed and out fell old bromides, ads scissored from other publications, a batch of company seals. I was about to gather it all up when he stepped in with a broom and swept it with the dust and dirt of the garage floor into a pile by the other boxes. We were finished by 10 p.m. I went inside the house for my suitcase and school gear. Then we drove Uncle Dirk's van into town. Helen's flat in Thorndon was down a narrow lane. Okay for a car—Helen's, say—but Dad didn't want to risk Uncle Dirk's van.

'He's a working man, Pete,' he said.

He fussed with getting the van parked. I had my schoolbag under my left arm and held the suitcase in my left hand. I had worked it out that I would shake hands with my right hand. Then what? Only that it would be done quickly.

The van shuffled its rear end into place. The hand-brake went on, and Dad said, 'Looks a bit dark down there. I'll help you with your suitcase, Pete.'

We could hear the clear notes of a jazz band from the tavern up the road. Dad said, 'Sounds like a sassy neighbourhood.' Not *Bride* territory, he meant. Then a little way down the lane, where the tall feathery toi-toi leant over the fenced-in courtyards, I could hear Helen's wind chimes, then I saw the Honda parked smack up against the door of what she said had once been a sea captain's cottage. Still short of the door Dad dropped the suitcase, and I backtracked a few steps to stare with him at the light through the front-room curtains. It was the only light on in her house.

'I'll tell her the van broke down, shall I?'

'Tell her nothing of the sort,' he said. 'When she sees you it won't matter. You'll be right, Pete.'

The wind chimes sounded again. I knew I should invite him inside, but worried that he would accept. In the end I said, 'Fancy a cup of tea, Dad?'

'Don't think so, Pete.'

He didn't move a muscle. Dad standing there in this bricked lane and the night dancing away from him with its sassy notes, mutinous as his own office had become and altogether as bewildering as Helen Jefferson.

'Did I ever tell you how your mother and I met, Pete?'

'Nope,' I said.

'Remind me one of these days,' he said.

I went to shake hands and he kissed my forehead.

'Kiss your mother for me,' he said.

He rang each day after that, always before Helen arrived home. We talked about what he was making for dinner that night. A couple of times Helen came through the door and she knew who I was talking to; her eyes grew wider, popped like the old days, and she seemed to look too hard at the mail.

'Your father?' she asked. 'What's new?'

'Chicken tandoori,' I said.

'Funny,' she said. 'He was always a meat and potatoes man.'

Dad rang twice in the last week of November. The first time to say he'd found a buyer for the house, and the second time to say he was moving to Brisbane, Queensland, Australia.

what we normally do on a sunday

My mother had known another man while Dad was away. Now that my father was back living with us she was trying hard to close off that chapter.

I was expected to know more than I did about Mr Windly and my father was disappointed that I couldn't shed more light. I loped alongside him and his gaze fetched off to the cool shadows of Hagley Park. He liked to walk holding his hands behind himself so that anything he might blurt could be passed off as an idle thought. Just an idea to float.

'Your mother says that Mr Windly would like you to visit. Apparently. What do you say to that?' I didn't know what to think except hurting my father is the last thing I would do. I was curious though. I couldn't think why Dave Windly would want to see me. He must have come to the house many times when I was there, asleep and unknowing at the far end of the house. I had seen him on plenty of other occasions. But they were fleeting and I was incidental to his purpose of visiting, and when I thought of Dave he was nothing more than a flash in the window. Sometimes my mother forgot to empty his ashtrays and in the morning I'd see them and know he'd been here in the night. My father gazed across a field where some kids were running a ball around. 'I was asked to pass on that message,' he said. Then his eye caught a red streak of a kite spiralling above the treetops. 'Remind me to get one of those. I think we should. What do you reckon?'

'I think we should too,' I replied.

His hand tousled my hair and I moved to his side, to his tobaccoey smell. His rough face grazed mine. 'We're mates?'

'Yeah,' I said.

'Forever?'

'Forever,' I said.

My mother worked part-time in a real estate office, typing, answering the phone. I often came by there after school so we would walk home together.

A few days after Dad told me about Dave Windly,

he came across the road towards us, blindly waving his hands at the traffic. He didn't seem to notice me. He had eyes only for my mother and as soon as he saw her displeasure he said, 'Ten minutes, Marie—that's all I'm asking.'

My mother continued to tie on her scarf. She snuck a look at me and decided she would say what she wanted anyhow. 'I thought we discussed this already, Dave. You promised me you wouldn't do this anymore.' She put her hand on my shoulder, and Mr Windly raised his hands in mock surrender.

'I'm not ambushing you. You're free to go.' Then he noticed me and winked. 'How's Harry? I know a place where they make the best milkshakes in town.' I looked up at my mother, and Mr Windly said, 'Hell's bells, Marie.'

'Ten minutes,' she said.

'That's all I'm asking for,' said Mr Windly.

The cafeteria was a few doors along from the real estate office. We were the only ones in there. My mother chose a booth towards the rear and sat with her back to the street. Mr Windly brought over a tray with a pot of tea and a milkshake for me. Then he sat down beside me and gazed across the table at my mother, and said, 'You're as lovely as ever, Marie.'

'Doesn't matter what I say, does it?' said my mother.

Dave leant back to get a good look at me.

'Harry doesn't mind a compliment passing his mother's way.' He laughed to himself and poured my mother's cup. Then he said, 'Do you still take milk or has that all changed as well?' My mother threw him a look and again he held up his hands. 'Sorry. Overstepped the mark. Sorry,' he said again. And he looked sorry. As he sat stirring his tea my mother shook her head at him. She said that he had to try harder. Mr Windly nodded like he really was listening and taking it onboard, then he reached over and placed his hand on hers.

'That's not what I mean by making an effort,' said my mother.

Mr Windly took away his hand and stuck it in his pocket. He shook some change there. I drew on my straw. I was beginning to feel uncomfortable because I knew I was in the way of whatever Mr Windly wished to say to my mother. In the end he must have thought he'd say it anyway.

'I want to meet him, Marie.'

My mother said he could forget that. Mr Windly didn't look like he was about to.

'I want to see what kind of fellow he is,' he said.

My mother looked at her wristwatch and Mr Windly reached around for his coat, and stood up. 'All right,

Marie. You know how to get hold of me.' Then he remembered me. 'Hey, sport, how's that chocolate?' I stared inside the aluminium container and squirted up the last of the chocolate milk. By the time I looked up Mr Windly was gazing calmly across the table that divided him from my mother. 'Marie, I'm not asking your permission.' He said, 'I know where he works.'

'God, Dave. You followed him.' Mr Windly didn't deny it. He picked up the salt shaker and examined it. 'I don't believe it. Doesn't matter what I say, does it?' said my mother.

'I'll wait until I hear from you, shall I?' said Mr Windly.

My father was dead against Mr Windly visiting us. It was night-time and I lay in bed listening to him argue with my mother. He couldn't see the point of it. My mother went on beating the eggs for the meal she was preparing in advance. I heard her say lightly, 'I expect he only wants to talk to us about insurance.'

'Oh sure, and I'm about to buy it from that fellow.'

On the night he turned up my father stood in the front room waiting and chain-smoking. I think he was nervous about what he might do. But all the accumulated hurt and resentment lifted the moment he saw Mr Windly pass through the front gate and limp up to the door. A cigarette hung from my father's hand. He stroked his chin and looked behind himself to seek out my mother through the walls of the house, wondering, I thought, how she could have taken up with a fellow old enough to be her father.

Mr Windly entertained with an endless supply of stories. He made my father laugh. At other, sneakier moments I caught his eyes following my mother about the kitchen. I thought my mother was aware of her effect. She smiled even when her back was turned. My father drank down his beer, then looked at the empty glass a little surprised.

Towards the end of dinner my mother took a phone call in the hall. At first Mr Windly and Dad waited for her to return. But she went on talking and finally Mr Windly said he thought he would have a smoke.

'How about you, Ross?' He pushed a silver cigarette case across the table for my father to pick up and admire. From where I sat I could see a neat round hole in it.

Mr Windly lit his cigarette, inhaled and turned his attention to the silver box. 'That,' he said, 'I removed from a German officer. The man was sitting at a table just like we are. Only he was dead. Though, I have to say, at first glance you wouldn't have known it. This man was staring back at the open door. A bullet had hit him in the neck. Must have bust his spine, I imagine. He looked irritated, like it wasn't the right moment for him to have been shot.'

My father began to laugh but stopped himself when he saw that Mr Windly hadn't intended a joke.

'His cigarette case stopped the first bullet. Or maybe it was the second.'

'First or second,' repeated my father. He nodded like he knew about these things even though he was just a primary school kid at the time Mr Windly came across the German officer.

'Sure, I suppose it doesn't matter,' said Mr Windly. 'But if it was the first bullet then you can imagine he was probably feeling lucky. He was probably halfway through congratulating himself when bang! that moment of irritation set in. There you have it. The roller-coaster fortunes of war. Probably why I found insurance such an easy transition.' He stubbed out his cigarette and lit another from the silver case.

'You own this house, Ross?'

'Marie picked it,' said my father.

Mr Windly looked around himself. 'You did well. It's a sound house. Decent neighbourhood. Close to the park.'

My father reached over and pinched my cheek.

'Good for Harry.'

'Sure. Good for anyone, I'd have thought.' Mr Windly leant back in his chair to look for my mother.

'She won't be much longer.'

'No. I was just wondering . . . two bedrooms?'

'Three.'

'Three's a good number. Nice and solid. A house is the biggest investment in a person's life. You scrape and save to pay off the bloody thing; you paint it, you look after it, hell, you come to love it . . . then one day, who knows . . . a fire or earthquake. Something happens.'

'The unexpected,' said my father, taking another cigarette from Mr Windly's case.

'That's it,' said Mr Windly. 'The unexpected. I think that about describes what I have been trying to say. The house crumbles. The very thing you've poured your heart and soul into. You can't believe what has happened. You can't believe it could happen to you.'

'Like the German soldier,' said my father.

'The German fellow. Hurt and confused.'

'Irritated, I thought,' said my father.

'And that,' said Mr Windly. He was about to say something else when my mother returned.

'I've been telling war stories,' he said, and for some reason it produced a look of concern from my mother.

'Are we ready for pud, then?' she asked.

*

We saw Mr Windly again after that evening. My grandfather died later that year after a month in hospital with pneumonia. The pneumonia weakened his heart and when he died he was at home tying up his sweet peas. There was a will and my father inherited his house out at Brighton. There were some Trust details, legal things that my father took to Mr Windly.

My father was building spec houses along Memorial Avenue out towards the airport. He worked long hours. At night he fell into bed and was asleep as soon as his head touched the pillow. My mother spoke of him as an absent stranger. She told me he woke from dreams in which he was hammering nails. He worked every day, even weekends. We hardly saw him. Finally, my mother said this was ridiculous; he might as well be back at Manapouri. Manapouri. Mere mention of the word brought forward a painful memory. Immediately, he cut back his hours and spent time with me over at Hagley Park.

One day in the park we ran across an old workmate of my father. He and Sonny Reardon had shacked up together on the Manapouri Project.

My mother stared back at our visitor—at his stained and broken teeth and the mane of grey-flecked hair brushed back past his ears like a woman's. He wasn't like the tradesmen my father worked with, men whose eyes and features she thought of as having been shaped with the right angles they placed upon the world all day and every day. Sonny didn't look like anyone my father would know. He was unshaven and his coat had lost its buttons. But I could tell she wanted to like Dad's visitor. For Dad's sake she wanted to like him. She went to take his coat and he held up a hand to say he would keep it on, and my father laughed out loud at the private joke that excluded my mother. I could see him watching my mother for signs of disapproval. He knew she wouldn't like him remaining in that filthy great coat. Now he watched her raise the glass my father had poured her.

'Here's to happiness,' she said.

'Happiness,' said my father's friend, and he added, 'because everything Ross said about you I see is true.'

My mother sipped her beer and went fishing with her sly eyes.

'Does that mean nice things?'

'Beautiful things,' said my father's friend. 'Beautiful. Many times beautiful.'

'In that case,' she said, 'you can come back any time.' She laughed and my father sat back relieved.

That night she sat with me in my bedroom trying to brush my eyelids shut and will me to sleep. It wasn't working because of the laughter coming from the kitchen. My mother asked, 'When did your father last laugh like that?' She sat there thinking. 'You know, Harry, I don't remember him once mentioning the name of that man.' She said the name over to herself—'Sonny.' We listened in the dark to them shouting names of other men they knew down at Manapouri. It was another world that neither I nor my mother knew about.

In the morning I noticed the door to the sitting room was closed. My mother came out to the hall and put a finger to her lip and I tiptoed past. The silence of the house felt heavier than normal. After my mother arrived home that afternoon she found the door still shut. This time she knocked and hearing no reply she pushed on the door and entered the sitting room. A cushion stuck inside a white pillowslip sat at one end of the couch. There was a smell of tobacco. My mother was sure she could smell that coat. She walked across to the window, pulled back a curtain, then changed her mind.

Around teatime the two of them tramped in the door with Mr Reardon's drawing materials, a bag, and a package wrapped in brown paper that turned out to be four cod.

'Tonight I make special fish in coconut,' he said.

My mother leant her elbows on the kitchen table and

watched Mr Reardon cook. She said, 'I don't think I've ever eaten coconut. It's not something that Ross would cook.' Only she enjoyed the joke. My father never cooked. Mr Reardon, on the other hand, looked like he did it all the time. His hands moved quickly, quick as blades, and as he worked he talked to my mother. He had lived in the islands. When my mother asked him 'doing what?' he wiped his hands on a tea towel, looked around for his bag and pulled out a sheaf of drawings. We thumbed through sketches of small boys tumbling over waterfalls. Sketches of the marketplace and Apia's rickety main street. The lush gardens. Villages. Portraits of billiard players, planters, Samoans. He said he'd worked in an ice factory but mostly he sold his sketches to day tourists off the cruise ships. There was one sketch of a beautiful girl with long braids. My mother held up the drawing. 'Hello. Who's this?' she asked, and Mr Reardon went back to his frying pan.

'Maia,' he said softly. 'That is Maia.'

My mother looked across to me to see if I had caught that.

'Maia is still in Apia?' asked my mother.

'No, Maia is in heaven waiting for me. Waiting for her Sonny.' He told of working in Apia's ice factory, and how Maia had never known what it was to shiver.

One day, without telling anyone, she walked inside the freezer at the ice works; the door closed after her and, as no one knew she was in there, she froze.

'Oh, that is so sad,' said my mother.

'Curiosity killed the cat,' said Mr Reardon.

'Yes, but I mean, to die like that.'

Mr Reardon glanced up to the ceiling. 'She is waiting for her old mate to show up,' he said. 'Of course, it is silly to hope. After all these years how would Maia possibly recognise me?' He looked over to my mother to see that he had her attention. Then he said, 'That is why I stay in this coat.'

'No.'

'Yes,' he said. 'It is true. Of course. It is so she will recognise me.'

He kept a straight face until her own expression fell into line with his. Then he burst out laughing.

'You bugger,' she said. 'I am not going to believe another word you say.'

My father's friend stayed with us for a week until he found a flat in town. We all missed him. My mother especially. She'd grown used to someone else cooking for us. The day he left we came home to a pile of sketches on the kitchen table. Some were drawings of my mother gardening and cooking. Others of me wrestling with Dad on the lawn. One of me on my bike pedalling for all I was worth. I looked so much like a boy that I was both pleased and embarrassed. Another of Dad with his foot up on a sawhorse smiling back at the picture-maker caught my mother's interest. She looked at the drawing for a long while. I couldn't quite see what she had found, but there was definitely something in that drawing that disturbed her. Dad's hair, the way he looked up from under his bushy eyebrows, his carpenter's arms falling out of rolled-up shirt cuffs. It was the something else that she studied, a kind of understanding, or closeness; something that approached a knowledge that excluded her. When she glanced up from the drawing she looked puzzled by the world as though in some fundamental way it had gone and changed while her attention was elsewhere.

Mr Reardon's place was in Montreal Street, a big old house with white-painted fire escapes—split into three flats. Mr Reardon's was on the ground floor facing the street. Without my mother's knowledge Dad put down two months' rent to get his friend settled. From a Colombo Street trader he bought pots and pans, cutlery, crockery, a bed, a bookcase and a lamp. He took some towels and bedding from home. I went out shopping with Dad and Mr Reardon, and outside a butcher's shopwindow the different cuts of meat caused Mr Reardon to stroke his jaw and wince.

'Meat's useless to me. It's too bloody tough . . .'

Over dinner my father told Mum he was going to give Mr Reardon some money to get his teeth fixed. As my mother was slow to answer, he said, 'You've seen how bad they are.'

When my mother failed to answer, my father repeated what he'd just said.

'I'm listening,' she said.

'You look like you're eating to me,' he said.

Without looking up she asked, 'How much?'

He told her how much and this time she laid down her knife and fork and got up to take her plate across to the sink.

'Don't say anything, Marie,' said my father. 'I only mentioned it because you should know.'

'You know what I'm going to say, don't you?'

'If we can afford to build a house out at Brighton we can afford to help out a friend with new teeth,' he said.

My mother's silence irritated my father more than anything she might have said.

'The world has a strange tilt on it these days,' he said. He stabbed angrily at a piece of potato but had not the heart for it, and threw down his fork.

'Damn it, Marie. You've seen his teeth. The man can hardly eat. Jellies. Milk. It's all he's up to. His whole bloody mouth will fall out unless something is done about it.'

'You didn't hear me say no, did you?'

'Oh no. Oh no,' he said. 'You didn't have to say anything.'

'No,' my mother said, looking right back. 'I didn't. And I'd like to think that's something for you to think about.'

Several days after the argument over Mr Reardon's teeth we found ourselves in Ormonds waiting in the usual booth for Mr Windly to turn up. My mother took out a hand mirror and checked herself over. She patted her hair. She said casually, 'I don't think you need to mention this visit to your father, Harry.' She looked at her watch. It was unlike Mr Windly to be late. She was thinking to leave him a note when he came in the door, shiny-faced, and full of apologies. He undid his coat and removed his hat and scarf before dropping into the booth.

'You look agitated, Marie,' he said. 'Agitated, but still beautiful.'

She smiled weakly, and waited until the waitress put down our tray and left, before leaning across to say, 'Now Ross is buying him new teeth.'

Mr Windly raised his eyebrows. He sat back, and I was sure I caught him sneak a look down at his wristwatch.

'No, wait. I haven't explained it properly,' said my mother.

'No, no,' said Mr Windly. 'I just wasn't expecting to hear about teeth.' He drew himself into the subject and asked why Dad hadn't just taken Mr Reardon to hospital.

'That's what I said.'

'And?'

'I don't know. There was some reason. His jaw's infected. I don't know, Dave. Talking about it now makes me wonder if I'm overreacting. Do you think I sound like a shrew?' Mr Windly picked up his teaspoon and stirred. 'Anyway, it's not just the teeth. Ross has outlaid left, right and centre. Rent. Electricity. Furniture. Kitchen stuff. Food. Our savings, Dave. What are we supposed to build out at Brighton with? Ross is just dipping in to support someone I never knew before. He's not even a relative. He just came here out of the blue.'

'Ross has a heart at least. I'll give him that much,' said Mr Windly.

'So you think it's me. I'm the one who's being mean.'

'Marie.' Mr Windly reached over and rubbed her hand.

This time my mother didn't take her hand away.

She smiled down at the table, then kind of floated up to him, and said, 'Dave, you should try to meet someone.'

'I have,' he said, and my mother waggled her head happily.

'I meant someone else. It's not too late, you know. A man like you. You should have children of your own.'

Mr Windly glanced around. As usual there was just the three of us in Ormonds at this hour. 'You remember the German fellow whose cigarette case I took? Well, he had a girl and two boys. There was a photo of them. The youngest was sitting in a swing. Sweet young thing. What do you reckon, Marie? Is he the winner here?'

My mother thought for a bit then answered in a slow, measured way. 'Not necessarily. Not yet,' she said. 'I wouldn't say that.'

Mr Reardon was recovering from the job on his teeth, and after dinner I went around to Montreal Street with my father to bring him soups that my mother had made.

Propped up with pillows, he listened to the radio Dad had given him. That's the first thing we heard out on the porch while Dad turned the key in the door. We tiptoed up the hall, my father calling ahead of us, 'Oi,

Sonny?' In the entrance of the door we looked in the darkened bedroom where Mr Reardon lay like a dying monk. In the corner of the room the radio purred with orchestral sound. Dad whistled. Mr Reardon opened his eyes and raised a hand to his aching jaw. Dad dissolved some aspirin in a glass of water and helped Mr Reardon into a sitting position. My father looked back over his shoulder. 'Harry, how about tackling the dishes?' So I went out to the poky kitchen. Out the back the upstairs tenant was pegging out some washing. Rain began to fall and she slapped her hands on her hips. She didn't know I was at the window watching her. I finished the dishes and went out to Mr Reardon's sitting room. The walls were pinned with sketches he'd done on his travels since he left Manapouri. These were sketches of the people he had lived among. Shearers. Men in narrow singlets smoking and playing cards. Fence posts and straining fence wire. Smokers. Sun-filled days. Years filled with wind and rain. Sun again. Shearing quarters. Frying pans layered with rancid bacon fat. Maori laughter.

My father came in. He looked at the couch he'd bought Mr Reardon, and with his eyes measured the doorway. 'Give us a hand with it, Harry.' Together we got the couch through the door into the bedroom. Mr Reardon's eyelids were closed; he was back to being the

dead monk, and Dad pulled the blanket up over his
chest to his chin.

'Come on, I'll run you home, Harry.'

My father stayed there that night. He returned home
the next day to collect some things, his shaver and some
shirts. He spent the next four days at Mr Reardon's. At
home my mother made dinner in silence. She hardly
spoke except to say it was time for bed. She asked me to
take something for my father around to Mr Reardon's.
I knew where the key was kept and I let myself in. I
could hear Mr Reardon in the toilet and it occurred to
me that I could get in and out of there without his
knowing if I was quick. I went through to the bedroom. Pinned to the wall was a sketch of my father
sitting on the couch, a blanket drawn up over him,
smoking a cigarette and smiling back at the artist. The
room smelt of sleep. The yellow light in the wireless
beep-beeped and the news announcer came on. One of
Dad's shirts hung off the back of the couch. It was like
a scene from home. Only it wasn't home.

Soon Mr Reardon was well enough to get up and
look after himself and my father came home. That
year Mr Reardon got a job at the Burnside abattoirs.
On Sundays he came round for lunch. My mother
made the lunch and set the table as if she was doing
it for strangers. Dad tried to coax her out of her

buttoned-up self. She said so little. Mr Reardon sat at the table grinning. Dad shrugged, and poured him a beer and Mr Reardon tossed his head back. He closed his eyes and for the time it took him to swallow it seemed he had left us for a place where he didn't have to try so hard.

I shut up about things which would have given my mother fresh cause for concern. She didn't know about those other times Dad met with Mr Reardon or his habit of turning up during our cricket matches. She didn't know about our walks in the park with Mr Reardon. She couldn't imagine what I saw one time after running ahead; I stopped to look back and was struck by the intimacy of their togetherness, the way their shoulders touched when they walked, my father with his hands in his pockets, Mr Reardon drawing a grass blade between his teeth, deep in thought. When my father glanced up it was clear that he had forgotten I was there. He looked at me for a brief moment. Then he called me over. He dug in his pocket to give me some money for an ice-cream. As I went to take the money he closed his hand.

'I don't know,' he said. 'Your mother will go off pop if she finds out you had ice-cream before dinner.'

'I won't tell her,' I said, and smiling he opened his hand.

He called after me, 'Take your time; there's no hurry. And watch the traffic.'

I crossed Riccarton Road to the dairy and bought an orange-ripple cone. On my way back I would have run into my mother had I not looked up in time. My father and Mr Reardon were off in another direction, sitting on a bench, and my mother had just spotted them. They didn't know she had seen them and my mother didn't know that I had seen her. It was an unpleasant feeling. It felt like we were all trespassing on one another. I left the park to make a wide arc so that everyone would see me coming and there would be no surprises, although my mother was gone by the time I approached my father and Mr Reardon.

The silences at home lengthened. My mother withdrew deeper into herself. It was as though she too had entered into the fabric of the secret and that she also had something to protect.

One Sunday morning she made a final effort to get through to my father. I say 'final' even though at the time I had no idea that it would prove to be the case.

'I thought we could do something different today,' she said. Since it was Sunday morning that meant passing up the regular Sunday lunch with Mr Reardon. I could see that same thought cross my father's mind but he was determined to show a cool hand.

'Such as?' he asked.

'I was thinking about the Port Hills. I haven't been up there for donkey's years.' She stood by, waiting for my father to object. She said, 'I was thinking we could take a picnic up there. Just the two of us. Harry can play at a friend's.'

'I can go to Michael Bevan's,' I said.

My father closed his eyes. He didn't have to say anything.

'Well, why not?' asked my mother.

'Marie, you know why.'

'No,' she said. 'I don't.'

'Christ, Marie, what do we normally do on a Sunday?'

'That's my point. Just for once let's do something different.'

My mother went and stood behind him, hoping. For a brief moment it looked like my father would relent.

'No. I can't,' he said in the end. 'You know I can't.'

'No, I don't.'

'It's the one high point in his week.'

'Then disappoint him,' said my mother. She took her hands off my father's shoulders, and waited.

'Marie,' he said. 'Where's this coming from?' My mother took a deep breath. She looked up at the ceiling. She wiped away a tear. Hearing that, my father turned around and took hold of her. 'Marie, what is this? What's going on here?' My mother closed her eyes. She swayed in his hands. 'Eh? I can't hear what you're thinking, Marie.' Then he said, 'He's a mate. I can't just let him down.'

'Let me be your mate. Just this once.'

My father didn't know what to say to that.

'I feel so alone,' my mother said then.

'I'm here, aren't I?' said my father.

'Yes. You are here.'

'Yes is right. My god, Marie.' He acted like he had just been given a fright. He looked around for me then. 'Your mother had me worried for a moment, Harry.'

'All the same,' said my mother. 'I think I'll take Harry up to the Port Hills.'

It meant that my father would have to make lunch but he knew better than to complain.

I hadn't walked along the Port Hills for years, not since Dad was away, and my mother reminded me of our favourite places. This rock. That patch of grass. I sat in a cockpit of rock and grass, my mother beside me. The wind made it like we were flying. My mother had to keep flicking her hair from her face.

'You can say anything. Whatever comes into your head, Harry. You're allowed to up here,' she said.

'Well?' she said a moment later.

'Nothing much. I wasn't thinking of anything.'

'I don't believe you.' She smiled, like it was okay, and immediately I thought back to that scene of my mother staring across the field to my father and Mr Reardon.

'You quite sure you haven't anything to say, Harry?'

'Nothing,' I said.

There were cyclists out on the road. Walkers. Families carrying blankets and flasks. The bus that had brought us up here passed with a new load of faces at the windows. We walked around two cars with smoking radiators. I felt my mother sneaking sidelong glances at me, waiting for me to say something. A hawk silently glided on the tops. To fill in the silence I started reciting the names of cars that passed us by. I knew them all. That one is an Austin Healey. This one a Morris. Now a Ford Zephyr. I kept on until my mother recognised one. Its blue-and-cream paint. Squarish windscreen.

'That's an Austin Cambridge,' I said, and to my surprise the driver pulled over. My mother bent in the window. She turned around and I saw she was relaxed and happy. 'Harry, look who's here. Mr Windly's invited us back to his house for a drink.'

The seats were firm. The leather smelt like new. I was secretly pleased we had run into Mr Windly. I felt like sitting, and it was a nice change to see my mother smiling and laughing on the road down the Cashmere side of the Port Hills. I looked out the window at the new housing. The clay still showed through the newly sown grass. We turned down a concrete drive and my mother gave a gasp at the monster house at the end of it. 'My god,' she said, and her reaction seemed to please Mr Windly.

The garage was under the house. This was the first time I had seen an arrangement like that, and we rose up a short flight of steps to inside the house. We bounced in there with birthday smiles, Mr Windly limping after us, holding the handrail for support. Everything smelt new. The carpets. The wallpaper gleamed. We tiptoed and whispered at the back of Mr Windly as he gave us a tour. We stopped outside the doors of two bedrooms and we peered in at the immaculate bedspreads. It didn't look like anyone had ever disturbed them. In the kitchen Mr Windly threw open the cupboards and the fridge for my mother to inspect. The best was last. The living room opened to a vast window, the biggest I had ever seen, which looked over town and the plains beyond. It was the same view I had seen from my rock-and-grass cockpit. When I turned around Mr Windly was smiling back at me. 'Follow me,' he said, and he led the way to his billiard room.

'What do you know about this game, Harry?'

'Billiards. Nothing,' I said.

'Or snooker. I prefer snooker myself.'

My mother presented herself in the door and smiled with admiration. 'This is so beautiful, Dave.'

'Isn't it just? Get yourself a cue, Harry.' He said to my mother, 'We can have that drink after if that suits you.'

'It does.'

Mr Windly limped over to a shelf and picked up a blue chalk cube. 'Chalk up, Harry,' he said. 'Most people only put it on after they miss. No one ever wants to blame themself for an error made.' I watched him set himself and draw his cue back. 'The idea is to hit through. Hit with confidence, I always say, or not at all.'

Mr Windly talked his way around the table. 'In this game you have to be patient, Harry. You bide your time until the other bloke comes unstuck. Then you progress through the colours. Yellow. Green. Brown. Blue. Pink. Black.' My mother ventured in from the door and folded her arms to watch Mr Windly pot the colours. He played his next shot and my mother laughed. Mr Windly shook his head and wondered how he could have snookered himself. 'Look what I've done here, Harry. Hairbreadth from that pot of gold and I go and snooker myself.' He walked around the table surveying the position from every available angle. The pink obstructed a clean shot at the blue. The white, pink and blue sat in a straight line, the first two balls casting a shadow. 'What a situation. What am I to do, Harry?' I had a feeling he knew exactly what to do and that he was just humouring me. He shook his head and tsk-tsked. 'Normally, you ask yourself, why didn't I see it coming? You think, if only this, that and the other had happened . . .' I looked over at my mother. She had lost her smile but she was listening intently to what Mr Windly had to say. 'There is a solution, however,' he said, and I noticed my mother step closer to the table while Mr Windly went on with his explaining. 'There is a practical approach and there is an imaginative approach. The practical man will play it safe, minimise his losses. He doesn't want to hit pink and give up six when he's only looking at four.'

We watched Mr Windly settle down to the practical man's stance. He set himself to play the safe stroke. His elbow went back with the cue then he pulled out of the shot. He dropped his trailing leg and straightened up. He asked me to pass the chalk. He said to my mother, 'For the imaginative man the prize is obscured but not out of reach.' My mother caught me looking at her and waved my interest off. She was blushing, though, and I was so caught up wondering about this that I almost missed Mr Windly's amazing shot. Without fuss, without even taking time to calculate the angle, he settled and drew a bead on the white ball and hit through. The white hit the cushion and nipped back behind the pink to collect the blue and deliver it to the side pocket.

My mother applauded and Mr Windly, cool as you-know-what, took a bow. He handed me his cue to put on the rack. 'I'm going to make your mother that drink I promised. I expect you will want to get in some practice.'

'Be careful of the felt, Harry,' my mother said.

'Oh, I'm not worried about that,' said Mr Windly. 'He's got a nice action on him.'

'Don't tell him that,' said my mother. 'It'll swell his head.'

'Some it might,' said Mr Windly.

I spent the rest of the afternoon knocking balls into the pockets. I tried over and over to bounce the white off the cushion like I'd seen Mr Windly do but without the same luck. I peeked through the door a few times. Mum and Mr Windly were in big comfortable armchairs pushed up to the window. I didn't want to interrupt them or to give Mr Windly the idea I was through with snooker, so I kept on knocking balls around the table until Mum came and got me. She said to Mr Windly, 'I think you've introduced him to a bad habit.'

'Here's hoping,' answered Mr Windly. He bowed his head and lit a cigarette.

'I hope he won't be smoking next.'

'Nope,' said Mr Windly, shaking his head as he exhaled. 'He can ruin himself on his own.'

My mother laughed and Mr Windly said it was good to hear her laugh again. Then he said, 'You know, Marie, you can visit again. You can come here any time you like. And Harry.'

My mother looked out the big window, for the moment smiling at something distant or an idea that had just slipped into her thoughts.

'Good. It's done,' said Mr Windly.

'I can't drive, Dave.'

'So what's the problem? I'll teach you.'

My father had concealed things from my mother. He had always pretended things were more complicated than they actually were. Mr Windly showed her things. The big one was showing her how to drive. To start with she gripped the wheel of Mr Windly's Austin Cambridge. I think she thought that if she loosened her grip the car would wrestle out of control. Soon she relaxed. Soon she was driving on her own. The car was the key. It enabled her to get out in the world and, importantly, escape that tight space occupied by my father and Mr Reardon. No one had said it was that easy. 'Fancy that,' she'd say, and that look of pleasant discovery was to remain with her. Foot down, nurse the gear shift, raise the foot and press down on the accelerator. Give and take—that was something that even a piece of machinery could understand.

It was that simple. From that afternoon on, my mother's life took a turn for the better. My father moved out the following winter. He and Mr Reardon moved to another flat. Eventually they would move to Queensland. By then, however, it wasn't so much a shock as a slight shifting of boundaries. Our own lives were undergoing subtle changes too. We were spending more time at Mr Windly's. Most evenings we drove up there. Mum would make dinner. I would have a round of snooker with Mr Windly. One night he said to me, 'Why don't you stop calling me Mr Windly? I think we know one another well enough now for you to call me Dave.' Then one night we stayed over. After that it just felt natural.

going to war for mrs austen

My wife would love us to be friends with the Laurensons —or for that matter, the Kerrs. It's a package deal, since we cannot befriend the Laurensons without the Kerrs or vice versa. Right now Jude is standing at the window. Since I came into the kitchen she has supplied me with a blow-by-blow account of the shovels and picks and backpacks shoved in the back of the Laurensons' Pajero. And now, for my information, she says, 'There go the plants. Tea-trees by the look of things.' Then she gives the saplings their Maori pronunciation—Kanuka. She releases the word slowly as if it is a new taste she is unsure about. But native saplings is the essential point, here.

This is something the Laurensons and Kerrs get together to do at weekends. They climb the hilltops around here and put up with the gorse clawing at their arms and legs to plant natives. Ross Laurenson has told me all about the colonising instincts of pines. How on windy days the pine seed is carried aloft to the native stands. From there, it is an amazingly short time until they gobble up the goodness of the earth and lay waste to entire hillsides.

I don't know what it was exactly but after that conversation with Ross, I just knew we would never be good friends. It was nothing he actually said—for the most part it made sense. But while Ross did most of the talking I just looked at him and thought, 'We're not ever going to be friends. Not good friends.' And that's fine. You can't be good friends with everyone in the universe.

Lately, however, Jude has been particularly anxious to know what I may have said to Ross that has left us without an invitation to join the Laurensons and Kerrs. She mines me for details. Specifically she would like to know what I said to Ross about pine trees. Was I in any way disagreeable? Tetchy? Look, my point is simply this. If she wants to plant natives why does she need the Laurensons and Kerrs to hold her hand? And, for that matter, I would say to Jude to just look at the

Laurensons. Sometimes they go off by themselves in their oilskin parkas and canvas knapsacks. They leave the house, holding hands, to ringbark a pine tree that has given itself away above the bush line. It's an honourable thing to do and I'm glad someone's doing it.

I don't know why I'm smirking; I don't mean to.

'We all stand to benefit,' says my wife humourlessly from her place at the window. She says, 'I admire what they are doing. If only more people were to follow their example.'

I throw the newspaper onto the table which means I'm gone. I have things to do. We've talked about the Laurensons and the Kerrs for long enough.

But before I disappear, Jude would like me to answer something.

She says, 'Before you run away . . .' and of course I hate it when she puts it like that—*before I run away*. What would I be running away from? 'Before you run away,' she repeats, 'I want you to answer me this. Can you please tell me what we believe in? I'd be interested to know.' Her shoulders kind of pop forward. 'I want to hear it from you. From your lips,' she says, which is to say that one of my long silences will not save me. Not today.

I start by reminding her who we voted for in the last election and the election before that. But Jude shakes her head. I'm way offcourse. She didn't mean that. What she meant is, 'What do we stand for?'

After some thought I offer 'Liberty. Justice?' And Jude gives short shrift to that. She wants me to be serious for once in my life. Just for this once, can we please have a serious discussion?

'Please, Tom?' she asks.

But here's the awful truth of it. I don't honestly know what else to say, which, in the end, is exactly what I tell her. I can't be more honest than that and in a perverse way I think it was the correct answer.

At first she doesn't reply. She just goes on standing there; her elbows are close to her body, she's thinking long and hard about what I just said. Possibly too hard, more than it deserves really. It's not until she lifts her glance off the floor that I see the tears—these are real tears by the way. I know because Jude isn't beyond the odd pantomime from time to time. But not today, not this moment. Those are real tears. I smile back at her. 'Jude, this is ridiculous. Crazy.' I hold out my arms and Jude buries her face against my shoulder. We rock like that for a while and I whisper, 'It's all right. Really, it's all right.' And it is, because through her cotton bathrobe I feel her begin to respond and, after that, we go into the bedroom.

But later, among the tangled bedsheets, she wants to

know if there is anything, anything at all, that I would be prepared to die for. Would I have gone and fought in Spain? Korea? Vietnam? And moving on, what would have to happen, politically, for me to join a human wall to stop the motorcade of the Pope? The American Secretary of State? Our Prime Minister?

I answered 'no' to the first questions and Jude, after hesitating, eventually said, 'I'm with you.'

I wish we could talk about something else. It's Saturday morning. I just wish we could laugh occasionally.

'You see, that's my point,' she says. 'We just don't care enough. It's a worry. I am seriously worried . . . about us.'

'All right then. Okay,' I say. 'We'll talk about it.'

But first I get out of bed to go to the kitchen to make us some coffee.

On my return Jude has switched on the bedside radio. Troops are parachuting in to the day-old sovereign state of Slovenia. There are reports of government troops surrendering to civilians armed with hunting rifles.

Jude is sitting up in bed with her arms folded around her. Her lower lip is drawn. You'd think she had relatives there—in the farmhouse that the newsreader has just described as being 'callously bombed'.

The thing I am trying to remember is whether she still takes sugar. Jude has an erratic pact with various diets. Sometimes she takes her coffee black, no sugar. Other times it is white, one sugar, two sugars.

I should have taken a punt but instead I make the mistake of asking.

'People are dying, you fuck.' She doesn't actually say this. Of course not. No. No. No. But it's what she is thinking. If only the guns were across the street, aimed at the house. Our lives would be so much more meaningful. That's for sure. We'd be out the back window, across the lawn and over the fence before the first howitzer blasted the brick side of the house. Instead there we are on this Saturday morning, unsure how to spend the rest of the day.

The news bulletin finishes with Elsie Harrow-Smith, who turns one hundred today. In silence now we listen to a young, fumbling reporter's demands to know why it is that she is still alive. Not in so many words, of course.

The wind has got up and we lie in that dark bedroom listening to the ghosts creak about in the ceiling. As the first drops pitter-patter on the roof Jude worries that the Laurensons and Kerrs will get caught in the rain. I remind her that they have oilskins. Furthermore, rain is the best time to plant a sapling.

'Ross Laurenson told you that, did he?'

'No. Your grandmother, as a matter of fact.'

This is her house. The original Austen homestead. Harold and Mrs Austen (I feel uncomfortable calling her anything else) lived their entire married life in this house and spent much of their time developing the gardens out the back.

Jude's grandparents kept separate bedrooms. We have taken over Harold's old room. The only thing in the room left of Harold's is an old mounted photograph taken of himself and Mrs Austen in Peru. You can see in the photo of Harold the slouching confidence of those used to having their way. He was dead by the time I arrived in the picture but Jude has memories of a pipe jammed in the side of his mouth, of his pianist's hands carefully arranged at the top of the steering wheel of an old silver Bentley and terriers jumping around the back-seat upholstery—on their way for a walk over the golf course or along the riverbank.

In the photograph, Harold has uncharacteristically given up the foreground to Mrs Austen, who holds a number of cuttings from an alpine plant.

Jude says the photograph was taken in 1947 and that they tramped three days to get to the location in the photo.

Another silence.

Then she says, 'Did you know that was the only time Harold allowed her to plant something of her own in the garden?'

I didn't know and, frankly, I find it hard to believe. My first contact with Mrs Austen did not start out well. I had only been back home a month and was probably too sure of my ability to impress. Mrs Austen had asked what I had been doing in America. I told her about the postgraduate courses in American literature and Mrs Austen said, 'So you've come back to plant a flag, have you?' Then she said, 'I don't detect any accent.' She had peered at the region of my mouth as if bits of foreign emphasis might be found on my teeth. She was pretty frightening. I find it hard to believe that she would have allowed herself to be trampled over by anyone, let alone pipe-smoking Harold.

'She hated Harold's roses,' Jude is saying now. 'She couldn't stand them. She said they reminded her of those silly brightly coloured paper rosettes worn by the party faithful and English football fans. She wanted to rip them out.'

'She didn't, of course,' I point out, and if this is an obvious thing to say it is only to remind Jude that the roses' survival would appear to undermine what she is saying about her grandmother. It is true about roses being Harold's life, his work. Harold's popular *Growing*

Roses for All New Zealanders was into its eleventh edition one year after his death. I suppose the thing I'm asking here is—can love for the man survive his work being loathed?

'Well if you must know, Harold was a bit of a self-centred pig, actually,' says Jude, rolling her legs off the bed. She throws on my shirt. I watch her retrieve the photograph from the wall. She still has a beautiful arse. As she climbs back into bed with the photo she gives me a questioning look. 'What?' she asks.

'Nothing. I'm allowed to smile, aren't I?'

For the time being Harold and Mrs Austen lie on the sheets between us, and Jude resumes the story. Some of it is new but most of what she says I've heard before. All the same I am encouraging and attentive. I'm just happy not to be bogged down in Slovenia or obliged to go over what I may or may not have said to Ross Laurenson about the pines.

There is Harold's failure to win employment as a plant explorer for a famous London nursery, his journey out to China in search of the rare Chinese pear tree, his ill-health and gradual recovery thanks to the selflessness of a New Zealand missionary family in Hubei Province, and Harold's ultimate arrival in New Zealand, where he meets Mrs Austen in the reference section of the Wellington Public Library. The rest of it

I know already—the purchase of this property and its transformation into the magnificent garden and show-place for Harold's roses and plants from the world over.

Then she says—'You realise it wasn't just the roses? She hated everything about Harold's garden.'

'Now I am surprised.'

'Well, it's the truth. The absolute truth,' she says, and for a brief moment we find ourselves looking down at the photograph of Harold and Mrs Austen for confirmation. 'You see,' she says, 'Gran loved Harold and loathed his garden. Hated it.'

Against my better judgment I put in a word for Harold. As I say, I never met the man. But there is the irrefutable fact of his garden, which was much photographed and celebrated.

I remind her, 'It was written up I don't know how many times.'

'That's not the point. That's not even what I am talking about.' She picks up the photo and places it on the floor beside the bed. Apparently I just have no idea.

'Come on then, I want to show you.'

'Show me what?'

'The garden.'

'I know the garden. It's the same garden as the one I woke up to this morning.'

'But I want to show you,' she says.

She jumps up from the bed. There's no way I can just continue to lie there. I am going to have to get up and go outside to be shown. As I reach down to gather up my jeans, she says, 'For god's sakes, Tom. Who's to see?'

She's right. The gardens have been cleverly screened by hedges. So we wander through the house to our overgrown garden. It is no longer true or fair to Harold to describe it as his garden. Even when Mrs Austen was around, the garden had started to run to wilderness. In the last year of her life Mrs Austen found eccentric jobs for me. She made me use Harold's old wooden tennis racquet to bat away the cicadas. She did not like the cicadas to land on her. So she would stand behind the screen door at the back and pass out Harold's tennis racquet, complaining, 'I can't go out there while the cicadas are terrorising. Harold, of course, would have used gas.'

It really is too cold to be out here without clothes.

'Take a good look,' Jude is saying.

The paths are nearly grown over. I remember a time I walked along them with Mrs Austen on my arm. By then she had decided that she could tolerate me. I remember walking beneath huge pink flowers encased in a prickly armour, on the end of thick green stalks. Something Harold had smuggled back from Madagascar. Desert flowers pierced the cracks in the path and rockeries. Black ground covers were used to sweat the soil and a misty spray from irrigation hoses managed to fool the tropical flowers.

'They looted everywhere,' says Jude. 'Mountains. River gardens the world over. They didn't know any better.'

Looting. There she goes again—a touch extravagant. I remind her of Harold's credentials and accolades.

'This is not my description. This is Gran describing her and Harold's activities, not me. I'm not saying. She is. I remember her saying it—they just threw everything into the rucksack. Whatever their greedy eyes fell upon. She considered the garden to be the result of piracy but Harold bound her to it. Even after he died.'

Jude wanders out to the start of the path. The gardens, as I say, are protected by tall thick hedges.

'Come on,' Jude says. 'Come and look at this.'

Then she makes a big sweep with her arm as if we have just broken into the tyrant's palace and are seeing hoarded treasures for the first time.

'Do you know what she called it? "A gaudy wallpaper of nations and national costumes".'

Jude says even her grandmother had found it confusing. She says Harold kept the garden the way other people keep a photograph album. In her final years Mrs Austen would stand on the back porch and struggle to make sense of it all. Smells and views got mixed up with the wrong continents. The garden had its roots in a maddening jumble of arguments and barely remembered itineraries.

'You know something, Tom? You know what I'm going to do?' Jude's not looking at me. It's a rhetorical question. 'Yes,' she says. Then, a second time, 'Yes' and a look of wicked delight lands on her face. She bustles by me. She's headed for the shed. I love it when she gets into one of these moods. Jude is really a lot of fun. It's the bloody Laurensons and the Kerrs that bring out this unwelcomed earnestness in her. She's so much better than that.

I venture up the path and stop. I can hear things being turned over in there. A moment later she comes to the door in Harold's old green parka. She has found a pitchfork and a cleaver-like tool that would be useful to beat back some gorse. I realise I'm thinking of the Laurensons and Kerrs.

She throws the pitchfork into the first garden bed. And—oh, I see what she is up to now. At the same time I'm not sure about this. I am not comfortable at all. And really I would much rather we talked about this thing some more but even as Jude raises the cleaver, I am struck dumb. It's only when she brings the cleaver down and breaks the back of a rose bush that I cry out—'Jesus.'

'It's all for Gran,' she laughs. But I can see that even she is a little shaken by what she has just done. She pulls some hair from her face and moves to the next rose bush, and then the next, talking as she goes—'I really don't know why it has taken me so long. I told you she hated roses. Couldn't stand rosettes.'

The cleaver is brought down. Another bush drops from view and Jude leans on the handle. 'The thing is, Tom, she couldn't tell Harold. Can you understand that? Tom?'

'I think so,' I reply, and it is true that I am beginning to see something here.

'Gran thought an opinion like that would be too much for their relationship to bear. And after all, she did love Harold.'

She is about to start on the next rose bush. She has raised the cleaver when something makes her return it to the ground.

'Well, Tom?' she asks, and this time it definitely is a question. Jude is simply waiting to see whether we are together on this.

And really there is no choice that I can see. It occurs to me that I am about to help in the destruction of a garden. I wish there was a reason not to. I wish its destruction wasn't so necessary. Perhaps it is the stillness of Jude's eyes or the way she holds her mouth that I understand—I understand all right that something is in the balance. Yes. That's it. Something important is in the balance. I am going to have to help. There is no way around it.

We work steadily. I have fetched from the shed Harold's old gardening boots and, while Jude continues to slash at the rose bushes, I work with the pitchfork throughout the morning.

Harold's rose bushes are lying on their side, perhaps as many as fifty or sixty, maybe more, but I have had enough. I thank my lucky stars that I never met Harold; otherwise, I am fairly sure, I could not have done it. As it is, by late morning I feel I've done my dash. I float the idea of a cup of tea and Jude says, 'Just this row.'

I am in the kitchen when the Laurensons and Kerrs pull up in the drive across the street. They pile out of the shiny Pajero. Their faces are flushed with good deeds. I imagine their legs are scratched and bleeding. I can almost smell the orange peel which although biodegradable is a foreign thing, and so it will have been conscientiously stuffed inside the pockets of their oilskins.

I attend to the jug and when I return to the window the Laurensons and Kerrs are looking directly back my way. A second later Jude comes into view. She is walking across the road in Harold's old green gardening coat. Her hair is matted from the light rain and her bare feet are red from the damp cold. Yet she is gallantly composed. Perhaps it is the green coat with its military overtones that makes me think of Jude as the cagey general wandering across the battleground divide.

She is beside the Pajero now; I have an idea Jude must have said something about our morning's work, because as one, they gaze back at the house. They look a little startled, then one by one they start to laugh. I have never seen the Laurensons or the Kerrs laugh before. From the distance of the kitchen I find that I am smiling—if not quite laughing. They look back at the house again and there is just time to step back from the window. I have an idea what my wife has proposed. There is just time to pull on my jeans and T-shirt. By the time I arrive back at the window the Laurensons and the Kerrs are following my wife through the front gate.

Warren was first into the water. He lifted his knees and kicked out over the shallow surf and dived beneath a breaker. Warren made it out beyond the breakers and lay on his back. Any moment now he would call out 'Marilyn' as was his wont when underneath a car and needing something from his toolbox.

We caught up to Warren—Tess, Bron and myself—and Mum, covering the last few metres underwater, surfaced next to Warren and surprised him with a kiss. Then Warren spoke up and said, 'Australia is out there.' He pointed with his hand and we tried to make out the exact place on the white horizon. Tess began to say how she couldn't see a thing—but lost the confidence to finish the sentence, or say it loud enough for Warren to hear. 'Yep,' said Warren. Australia, he meant. Our mother stared over his shoulder to the horizon with a dreamy smile, as if it had just become clear to her what the rest of us could not make out.

Well, Warren had seen what he wanted to see. Without a word he swung around and headed for shore, and the rest of us obediently followed. We picked ourselves up out of the shallows and wiped the salt from our eyes, and the first thing we saw was Warren sitting on the wet sand, pulling on the wet ends of his beard. 'Same old place,' he said, and to Mum as she bent down for the towel, 'I'm the abo with the spear. Watch out.'

We drove to McDonald's—Warren ordered nothing for himself which confirmed that he was upset, and at some point, either in the car or in the doorway at home, Mum kissed him on the cheek and said, 'Maybe some day.' But that was Warren, we told ourselves. Like a child when he couldn't get what he wanted.

Other times, usually after dinner, we drove to the end of the quarry road and watched in silence the sun deliver itself to that place Warren had pointed out, and felt ourselves to be fools for not following.

'Keith says formwork is a hundred-dollar-a-day job there now,' he said.

It grew awfully quiet. We could hear our own breathing. Finally Warren said, 'Yep. I don't know for the life of me why we need to stick around here.'

Then, a week later, 'How would the Musters like to team up with the Gilberts and travel over to Oz?' Warren happened to be cutting his meat, which he kept at as if nothing controversial had been uttered. We exchanged looks but were slow to comment. Then Warren put down his knife and fork, and got up to leave, slamming the door to the kitchen. We heard the car start up, and the spit of gravel as he reversed out to the road. Mum put on a brave face. 'Not to worry,' she said. Warren had got a bit antsy.

We travelled out to the West Coast beaches this particular afternoon, the last week in February. Warren was in a serious state of mind. Earlier there had been some shouting from the bedroom, after which Warren emerged and rounded us up into the car. I didn't care one way or the other, but, of course, choice didn't enter into it. It never did with Warren.

He drove faster than was comfortable. Every other driver was an arsehole, and usually Mum would have said something like, 'Warren, better late than dead,' but she didn't. He was in one of those kinds of moods.

At the beach he pulled off his T-shirt and kicked his

slippers inside the car. It was up to each of us to keep up—to get out of the car so he could lock up. He was in no mood to be delayed.

Tess complained of scorched feet so I picked her up and carried her as far as the wet sand. A bunch of kids were playing on a log, and a man wearing goggles swam side-on to the waves with a painfully slow crawl action. Every now and then a wave gently lifted him up, inspected him, and gently put him down again.

Warren dived and smacked his fists. He bullied his way out beyond the breakers. Further out he lay on his back, staring up at variable skies. None of us felt like swimming to his exact whereabouts, but since we were seated at the same table, as it were, there wasn't much else to do but look the other way. Mum had a race with the girls to hurry them along. We duly fell abreast of Warren. We were a good distance from shore but none of us gave it a thought. We had hit a warm seam in the current. 'Warm as bathwater, isn't it?' said Warren. And once to Bron, 'This way'—as if she had veered offcourse.

Mum said it wouldn't surprise her if we bumped into an oil tanker way out here. Bron immediately said she wanted to go back.

My mother laughed. 'Just a little further, Bron. You are doing fine. All of you.'

Then she put in a couple of powerful strokes to where Warren was shuffling along on his back. I heard her say, 'We need to talk.'

'I'm all ears,' he said.

'Not out here.' But then she said, 'Supposing we did, what about the children?'

I heard Warren say, 'We've been through that one enough times already, Marilyn.'

'What about Tess—her friends? And Bron? Jimbo just about to start high school . . .'

'New friends. New schools,' he said.

'Fine,' said our mother.

'Fine is what?' he asked.

Some spluttering from Tess attracted attention. She had swallowed sea water. So Warren rolled over on his back. He idled there while Mum swam back to Tess. She wiped away a trail of snot for Tess to say she wanted to go back. She was cold.

'Go back to what?' called out Warren.

'We're on an adventure, sweet pea. Yes, we are,' she said, nodding her head, I think to reassure herself of the idea. She called back to Warren, 'I've just told Tess we're on an adventure. Isn't that right?'

'Pretend. Pretend,' he said.

'I hate Warren,' Tess said quietly.

'Warren loves you,' Mum said.

Warren paddled his feet and blew up a spurt of water like a whale. 'That's right. Mollycoddle her, Marilyn. Every time that girl sniffles the entire company has to pack it in.'

'Tessa is fine, aren't we, sweet?'

Tess nodded, allowed herself to be placed back in the water under her own power. She put her head down and swam furiously, out past Warren.

'Dawn Fraser,' he said, now sitting in the water. 'That's another thing, Marilyn. We would have new heroes. More of them.' And he began to reel off the names of famous cricketers, tennis and league players. 'The Great White Shark,' he said, because he knew I had done some caddying before Christmas.

'Not to mention climate,' he added, and we stared out to sea.

Back the other way the beach had sunk from view. We seemed to be bobbing above the tops of farm scrub.

At last Mum thought to ask, 'What are we doing out here, Warren?' Her brave smiles had been deceptive after all. And of course. She must be worried. Probably she had been worried the whole time. But Warren pretended innocence.

'I don't know,' he said. 'You tell me. I know what *I'm* doing. Jimbo, what about you?'

I said I did.

'See? Jimbo knows what he's doing. What about you, Marilyn?'

Then Bron piped up that she didn't want to go to Australia. She was young enough to say what she felt, and I for one was pleased she had, even if it was just to say that she didn't want to leave behind her dolls.

'We'll buy more. Better dolls in Australia,' said Warren.

'But I want Hetti.'

'Hetti can come too. Jesus,' he said. 'What a party of sadsacks. Sing a song somebody.'

When nobody did Warren started to sing 'Advance Australia Fair'. He lay on his back as effortlessly as before and sang at the top of his voice. Barely noticeable at all, Mum had started to hum 'God Defend New Zealand'. Why, way out at sea, did I feel so embarrassed? In between Warren's bellows, we could hear Mum's fragile tune. I don't think she was particularly aware of what she was doing, at least not until Warren had finished and she was still carrying on.

'Well, well,' said Warren, as Bron joined in with breathless gasps. I could see Bron's feet and arms scrabbling to tread water, to stay afloat, and her face growing red with the struggle of getting out the words. I wished she would stop. It was a stupid thing to be doing way out here, without anything solid underneath us. At the end of 'Advance Australia Fair' Warren might have turned and stroked for the New South Wales coastline. But when Mum and Bron finished I felt as though we were all about to sink to the bottom, that there was nothing in this world to keep us afloat, other than this old Victorian prayer.

'You silly bugger, Warren,' Mum said then, and swam over to where Warren floated secure as a log. She was halfway there when Bron said she had had enough. She was tired, and was heading back to shore.

'Bron. Please, honey.' But Bron did not appear to hear. She was breast-stroking for the beach. Mum turned around to Warren, who was singing in a silly voice a few more bars from 'Advance Australia Fair'. He was enjoying himself—anyone could see that. Then Mum turned back to me and Tess. She said she wanted us to stay out here. 'I want us to stay together,' is what she said, but below the waterline I could see her legs quietly propelling her towards Warren. For the first time it occurred to me that her problem had become our problem. She reached Warren, and the two of them smiled back at us. Warren had one of his hands inside Mum's togs and they were looking at us, pretending that there was nothing for us to see that might cause alarm.

*

Maybe Warren was right after all. Even in late March summer hung on—women and girls wore summery dresses—a fringe of surf stretched to the white cloud, and beyond. There was a lightness here that included all manner of possibility, whereas, at home, everything had seemed anchored to the ground.

Warren's friend Keith, a man in shorts and desert boots, was there to collect us. He was pleased to see Warren. Tipped his hat to Mum. But the rest of us caused him to scratch his brow. Mum and Warren squeezed into the front; me, Bron and Tess sat in the back of the ute.

The air was bone dry, and Bron complained her eyeballs were hurting. Soon we were driving away from the city and the air smelt of bark and leaves. And suddenly of hot road mix, where we slowed for a road gang. Then for a long time we were on a highway. Driving to where—none of us knew. A few times Mum looked back over Warren's arm, which was slung over the top of the seat, to see that Tess wasn't hanging off the end of the tray.

Bron woke Tess soon as we hit the sea. We had entered a stream of traffic and were making slow work of it along a beach esplanade in the shadow of tall buildings. We stopped at the golden arches. Warren ran across for burgers and shakes, and we set off again, heading inland.

There were times in the days ahead when each of us thought we could smell the coast. Perhaps it was simply a longing to be where other people were. In the dusty quiet of the country it was a lot to wish for. Sometimes we sat on the porch and followed a red dust cloud across the flat scrubland, which traced the progress of a four-wheel drive. At night Keith put roo bars on his ute and from our beds we heard it smack through the undergrowth—the rip of rifle-shot, and the high whine of a vehicle held in low gear.

Warren and Keith went out shooting most nights. Friends from school it turned out. They took it in turns to hold the spotlight and shoot. Another man did the driving, a fellow from the Danish steelie gang with whom Keith and Warren were contracted to help build the retirement village—Ocean View—in the foothills. Warren sometimes returned home and reported having spotted the sea. On clear days it was possible—as well, it was comforting to know it was there; that there was this edge, that is to say, a limit to this new life of ours.

Our house for the time being was the former head-master's house in the grounds of an abandoned country school. We were saving ourselves a bundle living here, according to Warren.

Although Mum did say that she felt she would be able to chip in were we on the coast, where jobs were to be had cleaning out motel rooms and apartments. 'For that matter,' she said, 'I might even teach piano.'

I don't think Warren heard her. He walked to the fridge, took out two beer cans, and tossed one to Keith.

We were into our second month and everything that had been new was now familiar and practised. Warren couldn't think why Tess had to land awkwardly after all the times she had landed perfectly okay. Most times Warren slapped the side of his door and we jumped clear, like hunting dogs, from the back of the ute outside the school gates. This occasion the ute started to roll away, then stopped. Warren got out angry at the noise Tess was making. She was screaming and it was hard to know which part of her hurt. Warren stroked her hair and pinched her cheek. But it turned out to be her wrist, which he then held and kissed. He babied Tess until Keith called out something like, 'We're running late.'

But Tess was complaining that her arm hurt. Really hurt. Warren had another look. He gave it a waggle and pronounced it okay. He had done the same thing plenty of times in his younger days on the rugby field— it always felt worse than it really was. It was never more than a sprain which on the ladder of injuries was just a notch up from a bruise. And there was nothing you could do about sprains other than exercise patience and let nature take its course. At the same time he wandered back to the ute with a troubled look.

I think Bron, as much as myself, wanted to believe Warren. Tess was prone to overreaction. And already her tears had dried. She didn't mention it to her teacher and had no further complaint until that evening when she said it was hurting again.

Warren and Keith were watching the league on the box. Warren stretched his bare foot forward to the TV dials and with his big toe turned up the commentary.

But Tess was crying hard. Everything she must have held in all day was coming out. She hated Australia. Her arm hurt. And as much as Warren leant forward to concentrate he wasn't succeeding. Finally he had had enough, and yelled so he could be heard, 'Marilyn, will you shut her up, for Christ's sakes.' Then he shook his head and I heard him mutter to Keith, 'Every time you can bet your bottom dollar that little . . .' Keith wasn't saying anything. His eyes were stuck to the box. Apart from the commentary the only noise was coming from Tess. Warren shook his head again. This time though he got up and walked over to Tess. He stroked her hair. 'What did I say this morning, Tess? I said, "It's a sprain".'

Mum wondered aloud whether we had gotten travel and health insurance, which only further aggravated Warren.

He said to Keith, 'Can you believe this? A small girl falls over and suddenly we're looking at airlifts to hospitals. Tessa. Tess. Listen to me . . .'

But she was crying too hard. Sobbing her eyes out. Mum led her to the room where she and Warren slept, and Tess's sobbing carried on in there, through the doors, in competition with the league.

Warren returned to the sofa and sat down heavily.

'What have I done to deserve this?'

'I give up,' said Keith.

Then Warren noticed me lurking, and ordered me to the couch.

'The guy with the ball. See him? There. That's Bella. He's crunched through more bones than you've had hot dinners.'

'That would be true,' said Keith.

Then Warren said to Keith, 'It's still all new to him.'

I heard them shooting later that night. I lay with a sheet over me, listening to the crack of the under-growth and Keith's ute. It was going on later than usual. Mum came and sat on the end of my bed. 'Still up?' she said, trying to be jolly. A light from the hall-way found her face, a full cheekbone of smile that with a little prompting, I felt sure, might turn to something else. 'I suppose it all seems a bit strange. A new school. New country,' she said, and I knew she was waiting for me to say it wasn't that at all. She was daring me to speak her thoughts for her.

'Oh well,' she said. 'Tessa seems to have gone off all right.'

In the morning Tess was very quiet. She had no colour. It was impossible of course but she appeared to have shrunk, as if each tear she cried had contained a piece of flesh. She sat at the table with her bad wrist in her lap. Warren and Keith were still asleep, so we tip-toed around like shadows. After breakfast Mum told us to get dressed—she had an idea, and hurried us along to brush our teeth. We were leaving the house when Bron allowed the flyscreen to snap back on its hinges—and the fright stopped us in our tracks.

Out on the road the plan faltered again. Mum took Tess by the hand and looked to the road behind. There was no traffic for a hundred miles—at least that is the way it felt. 'Has everyone a set of legs?' she asked.

We walked along without making a race of it. The one car that came along stopped. The farmer was headed a short distance, to the store where we got our groceries. He was surprised to hear we were headed for the coast. Mum told him, 'We have a young lady here with an arm that needs seeing to.'

The farmer scratched his nose. He wished it were tomorrow. Sunday he was taking his family to Southport. Tell you what, he said, if we were still on the road on his return from the store he would drive us to the coast. Otherwise we might as well stay on the road and try our luck.

Luck took the shape of Keith's ute. It crept up behind, its fat wheels sucking up the tar.

Warren sprang out. A light joke on his lips, he said, 'Now where is this lot of nomads headed? Same place we are, I hope.'

Without a word Mum lifted Tess into the back of the ute, among the bits of animal fur and clotted blood from last night's shooting. She hauled herself in—me and Bron followed.

I barely remembered anything of the passing landscape which we must have passed all those weeks earlier. Tess lay in Mum's lap. Her hand flopped on the end of her wrist and she held it up not so much because she wished to show it off, but because it was more comfortable that way. Mum stroked Tessa's hair. Otherwise she was lost in her thoughts.

Soon we entered the outer suburbs. We struck the

first set of traffic lights and, after that, the malls. Again there was the sniff of the coast. A light breeze that we never got further inland. Bron said she wanted an ice-cream, but we passed the ice-cream parlour on the green light and drove to a newish building with tinted windows where Keith, I later heard him tell Warren, had been treated for the clap.

The X-ray revealed a clean fracture. Now that it was pointed out, the bend in Tessa's arm seemed obvious and we wondered how we could have missed it. Warren said he could have sworn it was a sprain. The nurses took no notice. If anything they were short with him—and Warren was asked three times by as many nurses how it had happened. Then I heard one of them behind the curtains quietly ask Tessa for her account.

The arm was to be set that afternoon. Mum stayed with Tess. Warren gave me and Bron ten dollars. He pointed out the hotel where he and Keith planned to hole up, and left us to roam.

That evening as we drove back towards the foothills it seemed to me that we were driving away from everything that was sensible and sane. There was Warren's work, and home, and no overlap, and no way of anticipating what was to happen next.

It was a week later that the ute pulled up early afternoon. Keith didn't come inside the house. It wasn't worth thinking about at the time—only a clue in hind-sight. Warren rough-housed his way through the flyscreen, gave each of us a filthy look and made his way to the refrigerator. He took his time in telling, and after he finished he sat staring at the floorboards.

The company developing Ocean Views had gone bust—or been placed in the hands of receivers—and for the time being cash was on hold. I didn't like the sound of 'for the time being'.

I heard Mum and Warren, later that night, making plans in the living room. Mum was doing most of the talking and for once Warren was listening.

'This is no place for children. How much have we saved up?'

'A thousand . . . twelve hundred,' said Warren.

'We will need a car. Not a ute, mind you, Warren,' she said. 'My children have travelled in the back of that thing for the last time.'

That was the end of Keith. We didn't see him again.

We bought an early model Holden. We tried it out first. There was a seat for everyone. Warren changed the points and plugs, rustled up a retread from some-where—and we were roadworthy, heading back for the coast, where we turned south, stopping along the way at building sites for Warren to go and enquire after formwork or carpentry. We stayed in camping grounds and did our washing in laundromats. Mum got work house-cleaning, so we would stay in a place for a few days—never more than a week—until we had petrol money.

It made no sense. Buildings were going up every-where, but at every site Warren went to the back of the line. Further south, and men gathered outside the sites; they sat on the fence like a line of still vultures, waiting for a job to come free. Whenever we pulled along out-side a building site, and Mum sent Warren across to the foreman's office, the men on the fence line watched without any talk in them; only their heads moved to watch Warren's return to the car.

'Guess what? Last month they wanted formwork-ers,' he said, getting back in the car. Always last month. I wondered how long, how much longer this was going to go on, and why we didn't just pack up and fly home.

Then one night we had to make a choice between somewhere to stay, and petrol; Mum kept driving south through the night, and the new day dawned in Taree.

Me, Bron and Tess untangled ourselves from the back seat, and sat up to find we had arrived in a park or public domain. We were parked on the edge of a field. Near a huge tent were elephants and horses. A man in tights walked along a rope. I looked at the map and found we were in New South Wales. The doors cracked as we tumbled out, and from the front seat Mum stirred.

Then we saw Warren coming towards us from one of the caravans parked in line. An older man in a white singlet and braces followed after Warren, who looked keen and ready with news.

'Wake up your mother,' he said. 'I think I may have something.'

But he did it himself; he was clearly excited. He leant in the driver's door and said, 'Marilyn. Payday.' He shushed up then because the man in braces had drawn near. Mum got out of the car. She tried to smooth out the creases in her dress. There was the matter of her hair too. I caught her sneak a look in the fender mirror. 'Oh dear,' she said. 'Heaven help me.'

The stranger nodded at her, and took each of us into account. Then he made as if what he had to say gave him no pleasure at all. We heard him apologise to Warren. He said he had misunderstood their earlier conversation. He had been so long in the circus business he had forgotten what a formworker was.

'I had in mind juggling, the wire, something of that order,' he said. 'But what you are about to tell me is that you're not a circus performer.'

Warren nodded, and studied the ground. He raked his toe back and forth in the grass.

The circus man seemed to be taking stock of the situation. He looked at each of us, again. 'Still,' he said. He twirled a finger in his ear, and while he was doing that he gave Warren a good going over. He walked around him twice, which is what Warren had done before buying the car. Now the man said he might have something after all. Mum smiled at Warren, and he took her hand.

Many years ago, in Italy, the circus man had seen a useful sort of stunt which he had, for some time, meant to introduce to this hemisphere. Maybe that time had arrived; but only if Warren, of course, was interested. Warren checked first with Mum. She nodded, and Warren was given the privilege of saying, 'Okay then.'

We were travelling north again, through towns we had passed in a single night—Port Macquarie, Kempsey, Coffs, Ballina.

Warren had his own tent. On its side was a picture of a strong man with curly hair and black moustache, and the words 'Man of Steel'. Kids up to the age of twelve paid two dollars for three punches to Warren's stomach. Clearly the man who had hired Warren had not been telling the truth. Bron and I had gotten friendly with one of the acrobats who said the last 'Man of

Steel', a Hungarian immigrant, had developed kidney trouble, and the circus had left him in hospital in Scone, New South Wales.

'Light hail on a tin roof,' was how Warren described his day's work. But at night our caravan reeked with the liniment Mum rubbed into his stomach and sides. Slowly he began to soften, like one of Keith's roo skins after a steady beating. The job was taking it out of him. No sooner were we in a new town and he suffered the runs.

At such times we left Warren in the caravan, alone, and Mum would take us on a walk in the strange town.

'Luckier than most kids your own age to be seeing the world,' she said. We didn't feel lucky though. We knew we should be in school, and in a strange kind of way it was unsettling not to be found out, or even to feel we faced that risk.

In Ballina, Warren said he didn't know how much longer he could keep this up. We heard him groan at night when he rolled onto his sore ribs. He had become a nervous man. The drop of a pin turned his head. The circus manager came to our caravan to say he was pleased with Warren's work, and to ask whether the kids needed something to occupy their time. Mum herded us under her wing and told the man the children were her concern.

'We want to go home,' Tess blurted, and the man chuckled. He poked his head inside the door and took it all in in a sweeping glance. 'This looks homely enough to me,' he said.

'Excuse Tessa,' Mum said properly, but the man waved a hand at her, and walked away.

'We will be out of here by June, Tess,' Warren said. 'June, I feel, will be time enough.'

We were prepared to believe it. We had something to look forward to—a means by which to mark progress. It was only three weeks off.

But June arrived, and nothing happened. None of us even had the heart to mention the fact of it being June. Not even Tess. We were in Southport, very close to where we had set out. Some of the terrain I recognised from the times we had ridden in the back of the ute. Not only had we lost our place on the calendar but we appeared to be going around in circles.

We had certain games and rituals to push ourselves on. At night, as we lay on our mattresses, Tess asked Bron to describe her teacher, Mrs Marshall, whose class Tess was to have started this year. Then she asked Bron to describe all the kids in her class, which Bron did, fitting out a name with a set of eyes, hair and skin colouring, and habits, so no two were the same. It ended this night when Warren sat up in bed at the other end of the caravan and sent an empty liniment bottle crashing against the wall above our heads. Mum yelled at him to control himself, and Warren slapped her.

I showed up at Warren's tent the following afternoon. I had to push through a flap and Warren looked up, saw it was me, and went back to reading his newspaper.

'Jimbo. What do you want?'

What I wanted was not easily put into words. A short while passed before Warren glanced up again and cottoned on.

'Christ's sakes,' he said.

'I paid.'

'So you paid, Jimbo. That's a dollar to the circus, and a dollar to me.'

It didn't make any difference, and he shook his head. He was leaning against a table, rolling back and forth a small pebble underfoot. Then he said, 'Never. Not in my wildest dreams did I ever think it would come to this.'

He looked up then, and said, 'What the hell. Let's get it over with. Three shots.'

He stepped onto a small raised platform. I tried to see him in the same light another visitor to the tent might, but I couldn't get past the fact it was Warren.

'Do you want the full works?'

I said I did, and Warren said, 'Okay, then.' He folded up his newspaper and slapped it on the table. Steadying himself he closed his eyes and concentrated for a moment. Then he started to recite with a strange accent, 'My name is Saffrez, last of the desert tribe of Assyrian strongmen . . .' I noticed his hands bowling into fists at his sides, and was concerned that he might be forgetting who had paid here. But he collected himself, and carried on. 'Hit me, the great Saffrez. And watch your sickly knuckles turn to dust . . .'

Warren's elbows fanned out from his sides and he tensed his stomach muscles. He waited with his eyes closed for the punch, for me to get my money's worth. Perhaps all along I had known I wouldn't throw a punch, but what surprised me was my total lack of desire. And at some point when Warren realised that nothing was going to happen, that he had tensed himself up for nothing, he sat down where he had stood. 'Christ,' he said, 'I never imagined . . .' He dropped his face into his hands. Then he shoved his hand out. 'Go away, Jimbo. Don't look at me. Leave me, please. Go to the beach with your mother.'

In the end I think we were glad to be walking away from it all, the yawns of the sedated lions, the pink candyfloss and the alcoholic clowns.

The shadows from the buildings had almost reached the line of dried foam above the wet sand. A knot of swimmers looking for excitement kept between the flags but well shy of the heavier waves. Me, Bron, Tess with her cast wrapped in plastic, and Mum, stuck together in the same channel, bobbing like corks, taking it in turns to check the arrival of the next breaker. There was no way out beyond the waves. No calm for a horizon to sit along like a painted line. Nothing but movement and foam as far as the eye could see.

And then, without warning it seemed, we were being dragged along a channel parallel to the beach, fighting it at first, then not bothering. None of us was unduly concerned. 'Look, Taranaki,' Bron said, of the spit of sand jutting out from the beach where we might scramble ashore. Meanwhile we did just enough to keep afloat. There was no question of us getting cold.

In time Warren showed. Mum was first to spot him by the parking meters above the beach. I think we had all expected Warren and were nervous at the prospect of him trying to wave us back between the flags to where he imagined safety lay. He was still in his circus outfit, and we watched this wild figure try to stay abreast, burning his feet on the hot sand as he stepped gingerly between the tidy Japanese sunbathers. None of us said a word. We were comfortable for the moment to just tread water. We were waiting to see if Warren would join us.

who's that dancing with my mother?

We were living in Napier at the time. My father pulled the keys down from the hook in the kitchen and my mother asked where he was headed.

'Up the coast,' he said, and my mother went on slicing the ends off the beans for the meal she now knew he wouldn't be around to eat.

'Allie,' my father said by the kitchen door. 'I feel like being alone for a while.'

My mother quietly emptied the colander of beans into the sink. She turned around to face us both.

'Just say where it is you are going.'

My father looked at the keys in his hand, and turned down the challenge. He crossed the lawn to the Hunter parked in the driveway. My mother followed as far as the porch. There she stopped, as if the lawn was a slippery area she would rather not cross, and yelled out, 'Why can't you say it, you lousy stinking coward?' My father settled behind the wheel and backed down the driveway. My mother raised her hands to her face. Then she noticed me; and that seemed to be the last straw.

'What are you looking at . . . goddamnit.'

From being hurt, she wanted to be forgiven. It was a confusing moment. Her face screwed up with anger, and she drew me over and said, 'Hug your mother, Charlie.' I was happy to, of course, but when I looked I noticed she had drawn herself into two parts: one I hugged, and the other—her proud face—had already turned with a thought to something inside the house.

I followed her inside, through to the living room. She walked directly to the bookcase, where she pulled out a thick book on flora. Most of our books were on plants, lichen and mosses. My father worked in the ecology division of the DSIR.

The book fell open, and the photo of my father fell out. It was taken near the snowline. There was no snow in the photo but you could tell from the rocks and the lichen grown over them that snow was not far off. My father had on his hiking boots. His arm was draped around a woman, an Australian. She was a plant illustrator, who had come here for dinner one night, a long time ago.

My mother studied the photo. She seemed to be trying to prise a bit more from it than the contents were prepared to tell. I couldn't say what she found. Perhaps it was because the photo was deliberately vague that she got so angry. She tore the photo into quarters and watched them settle over the carpet. My father's head was now severed, his whiskery smile even more of a mystery.

My mother stepped back and almost fell over. She had forgotten I was there. She swore, then smiled bravely. 'Know what we're going to do, Charlie? No. Second thoughts, I'm not going to tell you. Let's make it a surprise.'

Our town held few surprises, although it was useful to pretend otherwise. I was just as happy not knowing in any case, because we ended up at Chee's.

Some of the pub crowd had wandered across the road and were trying to chat up the Chinese girl behind the counter. The girl blushed and smiled out of politeness, but you could see she didn't know what the men were on about, and I thought it just as well.

We took the table by the window. Cars were leaving

spaces outside the hotel. One of the men at the counter came over and sat at our table. 'Hello, beautiful,' he said.

My mother turned and looked straight into his face the way it is said to be cruel to do with dogs. The man said, 'Jeeesus,' and got up as quickly as he had sat down. Our meals arrived. My mother hardly touched her fillet.

She counted out the money on the table. She had enough, clearly more than she had thought, because she appeared to be relieved. 'Now is the real surprise,' she said, and we started towards the beach.

The sea breeze was on the way out and the leaves in the trees along the esplanade had stopped rustling. It was growing dark, and sure enough the storm clouds were bunched inland over the ranges.

'I feel like dancing,' my mother announced. She looked at me, then burst out laughing. We walked briskly. The music from the roller-skating rink grew louder, and my mother pulled the sides of her cardigan to cover her chest. We could hear Cadillac Jack trying to hustle the crowd onto the rink. He spoke in rhyming couplets, so my mother said, and word had it he was brother of a famous American DJ. My mother always said it was worth believing anything so long as it wasn't harmful. So little happened around here, anyway.

My mother fussed over the skates like they were vegetables from the cheap bin.

She glided out onto the rink. She did a lap. Her lips were pursed, kind of hard-looking without lipstick. She usually wore lipstick when she went out. Her eyes were concentrated, as if trying to find a way back to some partially lost feeling. She came down off the high shoulder at the beach end and overtook a bunch of kids from the high school. You could easily be fooled, but if you forgot the rest of her and watched the skates you saw she was in complete control.

The third or fourth lap she came soaring down and picked me off the rail. 'Push off your toes, Charlie. Push. Push. You're much too stiff.'

She glided out ahead, and started to do a goose-step, holding one skate out front about knee height and alternating with the other. She came past the crowd and turned the heads on half-a-dozen cowboys. Her face glowed. She knew what she had done. She took off her white cardigan and tied it about her waist. Some of the slower skaters moved out of her way and found the sides as she barrelled down the straight past the hotdog stand. Cadillac, inside his glass dome, let go a ginormous *hoooeeee*. My mother went into a speed crouch and shot up high on the end bend.

Just short of the cowboys, a guy in black jeans and a

bush shirt tied at the throat with a length of string pushed off the wall. There were twenty metres in which to decide whether she would go around him. He held his hand out like a ballroom dancer. My mother dug in the toe of her back skate. The stranger's hand collected her around the waist; she spun around once, then again, this time under her own steam to show she enjoyed it.

They pushed off together, the cowboy holding her hand, and my mother bothered by a strand of damp hair that kept falling across her face.

I had stopped trying to skate. I leant against the rail in front of some spectators. I was wondering where my father was right at this moment. What he was doing. And what kind of person the Australian woman might be getting to know. I suppose I had taken over my mother's thoughts for the time being—caretaking while she skated.

My mother and her partner seemed none the wiser that a lot of attention was on them. The people behind me had begun to mutter. Something about the 'prison escaper'. Cadillac had gone quiet.

At the town end of the rink they rose together up the shoulder; the escaper hoisted my mother into the air. She threw her head back and used one leg to clamp his shoulder; the other leg she clasped behind the knee and held it straight out in front. In this formation they swept down off the bend. By the hotdog stand some of the pub crowd began to clap. I caught a glimpse of the escaper's face: it appeared caught halfway between a big loony grin and serious concern.

'I thought he had gone bush forever and a day,' a voice said behind me.

Somebody else said he had slipped out of the bush this morning. 'Robbie Hale seen him sniffing on the edge of town at daybreak.'

This time, as the skaters came barrelling down the straight before the crowd, my mother threw her head all the way back until her skates were over the escaper's head, which brought a gasp from the crowd. Then she brought her skates overtop, as if she was doing a backward roll. Over she went until her skates touched the rink. The escaper reached between his legs and drew her through until my mother was the lead skater. She turned to face him now, and he lifted her so she had her legs splayed either side of him and they were joined at the waist. People had stopped talking and were just staring. My mother's head was tossed back and she held on to the escaper's shoulders. She started to move up and down with her hips. Neither of them seemed concerned about skate speed. The escaper managed to steer them both up the end shoulder to see them down the straight. On the far side of the rink they moved through the pool of light from the overhead lamps, into shadows, then light again. My mother's face turned a fluorescent colour; now the escaper's head fell back. They were locked together in another movement that had nothing to do with skating.

I heard Cadillac come on over the PA to get more skaters onto the rink. But no one was listening. And there was no heart in the message, because Cadillac did not repeat it.

What happened next had nothing to do with Cadillac, or the crowd looking on. From the esplanade a police siren could be heard. The escaper's head turned a fraction. I believe it was the only intervention he would have heeded. He and my mother had come almost to a standstill in a shadow at the end of the rink. Some of the crowd had moved there to get a better look. The sirens were close now. My mother was lowered onto her skates. She and the escaper stood straight and near to each other, like lovers in a park.

He kissed her once—on the cheek. Then he split. He pushed off and was nearly in a speed crouch when he passed me.

I heard someone bitch that the escaper hadn't returned his skates. 'Typical,' from someone else.

He leapt the turnstile for the esplanade and skated

through the first set of lights. One violation after another, cast behind like discarded clothing.

My mother was buttoning her cardigan, as if it was the most important thing in the world. Her cheeks were still flushed. She knew I was nearby, but she looked up in her own good time. She said, 'You enjoying yourself, Charlie? Not too much, I hope, because I feel like going home now.'

The drunks near the hotdog stand called out things, but she took no notice. 'Look at that, Charlie,' she said, and very deliberately she pointed over the heads of the cowboys, to a fairly ordinary sunset.

While we were getting out of our skates Cadillac came out of his glass dome. I had never actually seen him. He had a pointed beard—like the famous record-spinner—but he only just cleared the top of my head. He looked frightened, and in a quiet voice I never imagined might be his he said the police had sent through word that they wished to speak with my mother.

He mentioned the man being an escaper, and my mother, still cool as a cucumber, said, 'What, you mean that nice young man?'

Two blocks away from the skating rink she permitted herself to say something, and I realised she was shaking like a leaf.

'I feel like singing,' she said to the trees. Then she stole a quick look at me. 'Charlie, you're not angry with me. Are you, Charlie? Don't be. I haven't skated like that for years.'

We came to our street and from here we should have been able to see the house lights. The car wasn't in the driveway, and I worried that it would have some effect. But she didn't appear to notice. Or, if she did, she didn't care. At the door she said she thought she might have a bath. As it happened we pushed through to the living room, where her eyes went straight to the torn quarters of the photograph. She crossed her arms, and thought.

'Charlie,' she said. 'Go get that glue from the top of the fridge. Let's not disappoint your father.'

one

Naturally they want to know how it all started. They observe that I was once a raindrop.

'Yes, briefly.'

'And let's see, you were once a sheep?' They push their glasses' frames another notch down their noses and look up. This is an invitation for me to back down and reveal my lighter, frivolous side.

Instead I say, 'Mary.' That's who I was seeing at the time.

'And you've been a sparrow, a knife and fork, Henry Ford? A wood pigeon? You know,' they say, 'there are people out there who believe you are a danger to yourself. I mean, really, a sparrow?'

Of course I'm being provocative. After all—a knife and fork, and Henry Ford for god's sake. Though when they mention the sparrow I usually try to explain. 'It's not what you think. Everything is a tight fit and light all at once. A bit like being high.'

Each interview is like every other one. My interrogators come here as doubters and pretty soon they are hunched forward on the edge of their seats saying, 'No, really?' and 'Would you mind telling us a war story?'

Of course it is not my war story, you understand. But it goes like this.

I am a GI and I have just burst in to Hitler's bunker. He is not dead. He is alive. I repeat—alive. He is looking up the barrel of my gun. Black eyes. Moustache. He is saying, 'I will give you chewing gum. Do you like Juicy Fruit? No, let me guess. P.K? Arrowmint?' I'm thinking, Nobody is going to believe this, and, He's the guy who killed the Jews. I find myself reaching for the Arrowmint when, thank goodness, Sergeant Hawk bursts in with a hand grenade in each hand. Hawk always knows what to do in these situations.

'Blow the fucker, boy,' he says.

Then, years later. This is still the same story. Only now I am seventy-three years old. I have grandchildren, and whenever Hitler comes on TV, I want to say, 'There's the guy who tried to give me a piece of gum.' I don't though. Lord, no. I keep my trap shut, because the last thing I want is to give them an excuse to run me out to the old people's home. Hitler is on TV again, but I don't say anything, and it is the most god-awful frustrating thing in the world.

The magazine writers have usually done their homework. And, although I expect their question, I still don't have a convincing response.

They note that I was once a writer.

Up to now I have been a wise old head; now they see an embarrassed shopkeeper before them. They sense they have scored a point and sit back in their chairs chewing their pencil ends.

I never thought I would become a shopkeeper. I had my heart set on a different club altogether. Balzac. Dickens. I grew up reading their books, and from the moment I first held a pencil I was trying to circle bits of the world and colour them in. I dreamt of contributing wonderful lives, superior lives. There was a time in my life when I would gladly have given up everything to bring another Pickwick into the world, or to register perfectly the colour and taste of love and revenge.

For a number of years I toiled away at my stories. But did anyone ever read them? The question was too terrifying to ponder for long. In moments of clear-headedness, though, I saw my efforts as cast-off matter, simply as proof of industry—at best, proof of a lonely discourse between me and the flickering screen. I began to blame the book, the thing itself. I developed conspiracy theories—but best I don't go into these. Suffice to say I was ready to explore other possibilities.

I decided to take my characters out into the world— let them loose on a larger population. I took my impersonations to the pub—the Arms, the Cricketers, the Coachman. A distinctly unliterary audience: bodies swollen with piss and wind, firing questions back at President Kennedy's driver and Henry Ford. It's funny what works where—Kennedy at the Arms but not the Coachman, my knife-and-fork act at the Post but not the Bond. Whereas Sergeant Hawk and Hitler's bunker go down well just about anywhere. The old soldiers come up to me afterwards and want to buy me a pint.

two

I think it was the Arms where Neil Owen collared me. I didn't notice him until the end of the evening. He stood by himself at a distance, without a drink in his hand. Sober too, which gave him a certain distinction.

He waited until the old soldiers dispersed before coming forward.

I suppose he was in his late thirties, perhaps a little older, though still with a country boy's eyes—and shy, that much was clear. He'd patiently waited to get my attention and now he had it he didn't know what to do with it. 'I enjoyed the show,' he said. I thanked him and turned to leave. 'Actually, I've come to ask for your help.' I stopped and when I turned around he offered his hand. 'Neil,' he said. 'Neil Owen.'

'We'll sit down, eh, Neil, and you can tell me what this is about.'

It was difficult for him to spit it out. He released his story—a bit at a time. It seems Neil's wife had developed an alternative world for herself. An imaginative world. A private kingdom with high walls that prevented him seeing over. This was better than I might have expected, more rewarding than listening to the war stories of old soldiers with their flies undone and the corners of their lips cracking open with spittle.

So far so good. Neil spoke about their market garden venture and I imagined a flat bit of dirt with big puffy clouds rolling over the top. He said, 'We spend a good deal of time alone with our thoughts. Until recently I would have been the first to say that where Judith goes with her thoughts is her own affair. Until very recently, that is.' He looked up with hurt eyes. 'My wife is in love with a fellow over in Russia.' He watched me, gauging the effect of his words.

I nodded. 'Go on,' I said.

'She dreams about Russia constantly. She spends half her time there. One time when Judith was there, she was raped, then this other fellow picked her up and took her home. As far as I know she's still with him. I don't know for sure: she's clammed up recently. I'm pretty sure. Well, more than sure.' He paused there and released a big breath. He looked up at the ceiling then back at me. 'You're the first person I've told this to. By the way, I lied before. This isn't the first time I caught your act. I wasn't sure, you see, so I had to come again . . .'

We talked for the next hour. He went back to the beginning and described his wife's obsession with things Russian. It had started innocently enough over the winter with her reading a pile of Russian novelists. At first she tried to involve him—reading aloud to share a sentence she felt he might warm to. Gradually, over time, the shelves lengthened with Russian novels and soon she began to dream of Russia. At night Russia was vividly real, unbelievably real. In the mornings she encouraged Neil to put on a ski mask and stand out in the orchard to grasp the texture of Russia. She has told him it is grey with lovely swatches of eye shadow, reds, blues and lighter tones. He put on the ski mask to humour his wife and thought nothing of it.

Then one night his wife lurched awake. Her pyjama top was wet through. Her face was covered in a filmy sweat. He watched his wife's fingers collect and uncollect. Then her eyes spilt open.

'Neil?' she asked.

'I'm here,' he said, and instantly her face relaxed.

She lay back in bed and closed her eyes. 'My god,' she said.

He leant across and placed his hand on her thumping chest. Then, for the next twenty minutes or so, Neil was the policeman taking down notes as Judith reported back her Russian experience.

Up to now, Russia had been a sunny place—without any dark clefts. But on this night she arrives to a murderous atmosphere rolling through a Jewish neighbourhood. People are fleeing by her. Windowpanes burst onto the street. There are shouts, screams, the whinnying of horses driven into tight spaces. Mattresses have been dragged outdoors and slashed. White feathers lie all over the street. Wading through them is a proud but mute woman: she holds her blouse wide to show the world where her chest has been treated like tree bark for her attacker to carve his initials. An old man staggers out a doorway carrying his bearded head in his hands, blood fountaining out an open neck.

Still, Judith is at the safe remove of the tourist. She is there but not really there. She is wondering where to go next when an older woman takes hold of her elbow and guides her through a cottage to a courtyard. The woman seems to know what to do and when she pauses to gather up a lost kitten Judith is reassured by her composure. They climb a ladder to a loft where they arrange themselves face-down on the floorboards. After a few minutes the ghastly violence sweeps underneath them for another street.

Judith paused there, and Neil, thinking it was the end of her account, got up to make them both a cup of tea.

Judith didn't sleep that night. She fidgeted beside Neil until he too lay looking up into the dark—the two of them kept awake by events in Russia.

A day passed. Judith was planting tomatoes. Burying the trowel and pulling the earth to one side, inserting the plant. Neil walked over to his little farm machine, crouched behind her to stroke her bare arms. He said to her, 'Judith, can we go back to the other night, that moment you are in the loft . . .'

She paused from the trowelling, allowing her thoughts to catch up with the request. Then she stood up and looked him squarely in the eye. 'Just remember,' she said, 'you were the one who asked.'

Back to the loft they go. At the sound of the glass breaking in another neighbourhood, she and the other woman raise their heads and look at each other, as if to ask, 'Is it safe?' Judith, for one, has had enough. She wants to get out of Russia and return to the Wairarapa. In the loft, the righteous indignation of the tourist has been fermenting inside her. Now, she thinks, if she stands up to the window she will see the gummy hills of home. She is utterly convinced. And when the other woman hisses at her to stay down, Judith smiles confidently in the knowledge of what she knows.

As she approaches the window, Russia comes bounding back into view. Apparently there is no way out. She is the marooned tourist everyone has read about and fears themselves becoming—trapped behind unfriendly borders without a passport, without a visa, without the language to negotiate. Down in the street she sees the Moldavians wiping their bloody knives. At that moment the kitten miaows and a boy of about ten looks up. Briefly, their respective worlds teeter and shift, and then the boy's eyes begin to narrow and Judith distils his thoughts—his father has promised to reward his alertness with a toy. Her life is about to be traded for a toy soldier. Slowly, the boy raises his finger. One by one, the Moldavians withdraw from their conversation and look up. After a brief consultation, a number of them start for the loft; she can hear them coming up the ladder, their knives and hammers banging against the wood.

The rest of it—the rape—she refused to go into. Although she did admit to Neil that even as the Moldavians were climbing the ladders she had this idea that she would still be all right. She would explain that she was a New Zealander and after that everything would be set right. The mob would apologise and bashfully retreat. 'However ...' she said, and she moved on to afterwards, to that moment when a hand cups her groin and she is being turned upside-down, to when she is free-falling. The street races up, she feels its hard shoulder and glimpses the sky reeling away.

That afternoon Neil took himself off to the library. He cycled all the way into town, to the Sea Breeze Arcade. There's a video store, a coffee lounge whose proceeds go to cancer research, a travel agent's office that is haunted—with a man grown pale who sits behind a dull window all day stirring sugar into his coffee.

As Neil described this, I was thinking, Well, there's the problem in a nutshell. It has to do with where they live. Judith is bored out of her mind. The two of them are going crazy in the childlessness of their days and nights. Too preoccupied with themselves, is my theory. Still, I don't say anything.

In the library Neil asked for books on Russia, and the librarian suggested he look under *Poetry & War*. He flicked through some poetry. Snow, crows, the birch trees in winter, exile. In the *Large Books* section he pulled down a volume of photographs of Soviet industrial achievement up to 1933—one photo showed a pyramid of men, each one standing on the shoulders of another, to paint the vast face of a newly built dam. No sign of Judith's Russia there.

Days, weeks passed. Then one night Judith came forward with fresh information that advanced the story. There was the rape, and later she was thrown from the loft and left for dead. Here's what she told Neil.

When she gains consciousness she finds herself in quiet surroundings. In this strange bed, in someone else's bedclothes. She is aware of chickens pecking outside the window by her bed. In the upper part of the window she can see a line of black crows looking in from the bough of an old walnut.

She told Neil a doctor bathed her. A kind and gentle soul, she called him.

The doctor organises a servant to heat up some water. Then, when the water is ready the doctor and servant help her from the bed. The doctor rolls up his sleeves. He kneels beside the bathtub and asks Neil's wife to turn her knees into mountain peaks.

'This way, my little bird,' he says, washing one leg, then another.

'What else?' Neil asked. 'Did he soap all of you?'

'He helped to bathe me, yes.'

'Your breasts?'

'Of course,' said Judith. 'My breasts are part of me.'

'And down there?'

'Neil. For god's sake.'

'And he called you "my little bird"?'

'All right. That's it,' she said. 'I'm turning out the light.'

But Neil, anxious to get to the bottom of this, persisted, 'How many times has he bathed you, over there, in Russia?'

'I'm turning out the light, Neil. I'm switching it off.' And then, needlessly, as he reports it, 'The light is out.'

three

'Can you help me?' Neil leant across the table in the pub. 'Just one night—that's all I ask—to slip into her dreams.'

He saw me look towards the door.

'There's no one else I can turn to,' he said.

But could I help him? That's what I was wondering.

It is winter in Russia. The oak tree outside the window has long since shed its leaves. At night when the air temperature sits on freezing, Neil's wife and the doctor huddle by the wood burner.

Over in the Wairarapa it was the planting season, and there were plenty of days when Neil would look up from the row he was planting to find his wife's smile closed around this other world from which he was excluded, a place where bells ring from horses' necks, and sledges whistle through the snow.

The bathings—this routine of theirs—have become more regular than Neil would wish for, the doctor's childish game masking a more serious intent. Neil was amazed his wife couldn't see through it. Such as the doctor asking for the hilltops to rise so he can slide his soapy hands beneath the full weight of her breasts. Or when he says, 'Please. Show me your steppe,' and she obediently raises her flat white belly above a layer of foam for the doctor's hands to wander and explore. To distract attention from his prying he hums popular Russian folksongs.

Each morning the doctor intercepts his servants

with the breakfast trolley—'Ah, what have we here?'—treating it as through it was a chance encounter, no more, and proceeds to Judith's room. He is always delighted to see her. He sets about arranging her pillows. 'How is my little bird today?' Today he has a gift for her, a nightgown. Tomorrow it will be honey, or a jar of marmalade.

Twice now Judith has attempted to discuss with the doctor the attack on the Jewish neighbourhood. Both times he placed a finger to his lips. Once he popped a spoonful of yoghurt in Judith's mouth. The second time he scraped a smear of honey from her cheek then held his finger a few inches above her mouth until she came up to taste it. 'There. There. My baby golubchik.' And he made the cussacking sound of a dove.

And there was more. Last night, said Neil, a name bubbled from his wife's lips. Mikhail.

I had to admit the very sound of the name was discouraging. Mikhail—the word opens the mouth. It makes space for and leaves behind a certain yearning.

Neil must have detected in my expression some lingering doubt, for now he produced a chequebook and laid it on the table between us.

'Of course,' he said, 'you have your expenses to consider.'

four

Think of the sun staring at the earth, of it frowning through the clouds, alternating with periods of concentrated effort, day after day willing the seed to burst from the unseen world into the open. And you get an idea of how Judith's Russia was able to flourish and take over the life she led with Neil in the Wairarapa.

The imagination can turn into a blunt instrument without something to react against. The imagination loves to be pandered to, loves attention. I began my work for Neil by reading around the subject. I read Russian folktales, I studied maps, I thumbed through the country's history in order to dream up stories to enable Neil to burrow through to Mikhail's neighbourhood. We met once or twice a week and, for want of a better description, I came to think of these occasions as Neil's lessons.

I planted stories in his imagination, I scoured the town for Russian landscapes, I dreamt up people. Early in the piece I drew him over to my window to point out 'my Russian neighbour' and Neil gazed back at Trisha Blake weeding her garden.

'There's your Russian, Neil. In case you've never seen one before.'

Neil shook his head, willing the little he knew of

Russia to take seed in dear old Trish. 'Yes. Interesting,' he said. 'I mean, you wouldn't know but for that thick neck, and, oh, yes, the headscarf sort of gives her away, doesn't it?'

Point number one: the imagination is non-discriminating when it comes to old prejudices and lies.

'Masha Venyukova. That's her name,' I said.

Point number two: in stories we trust. We ask no questions. In stories we glimpse other possibilities. I began to load Trish with character, background, history. I sweated it to begin with, and sketched Masha Venyukova as I went. What writer has to put up with a reader looking over their shoulder as they advance the story? Back then I was not the practised adlibber I've since become. Several times I had to excuse myself to go to the toilet or out to the kitchen for another glass of water, to give me a moment to invent away from Neil's trusting eyes.

Russian lessons. That's what they were. Neil even took notes and I brought out my maps to locate Odessa on the Black Sea. He stood at the window while he listened to me, holding back the curtain and looking down at the crouched figure of Masha Venyukova.

'Odessa? That's where she's from?'

'No,' I said. 'Odessa is where the circus business regularly took her. She was a procurer of circus acts.'

Neil mouthed a silent 'Ah'. Then he asked, 'She told you all this?'

'We're great mates. But listen,' I said. 'This is what I wanted to tell you. This is what she told me.'

On one of her trips to Odessa she gets word of a very special exhibit down in the port. From the top of Potyomkin Steps she can see the white rust-bucket which had ferried the Turk and his wares across the sea. It is a hot day and she toys with stopping at a cafe but, as she is already late, she continues to drop down the steps, past the sailors' bars and the tired, unpainted entranceways of the prostitutes' quarters. She hurries across the busy port road, through the gates, and finds the Turk's ship. She takes off her shoes and climbs the gangway. At the stern, a small crowd of her circus colleagues has gathered. But she is already late—the auction is underway.

In fact, when the Turk announces he will introduce his wife, she thinks it must already be over. But as is his practice, the Turk has left the best for last. He disappears briefly and returns with what appears to be a mannequin in a black dress and black stockings.

Masha thinks the woman must have died recently—leukaemia, possibly, or TB—and that the impresario, under mounting financial pressure after a recent flop with his Russian-speaking ponies, has taken his wife to a taxidermist who has removed the brain and intestines and filled the body with an aromatic resin.

'So she bought the Turk's wife?' asked Neil.

'No, she did not. Her bid wasn't successful.' Though, god knows, she was deeply sorry to have missed out, as procurers of circus acts received appalling pay.

Now, with the auction over, the Turk kisses his wife goodbye. Masha sees him afterwards standing at the ship's rail, a bald man with a sad, down-turned moustache, a hand raised in farewell to his wife of thirty years, as another, a fellow from a Romanian circus, carries the corpse wrapped in brown paper past the wharf authorities.

By now it is late afternoon, still very warm. Rather than return to the hotel, Masha wanders Odessa's leafy streets. She keeps to the shaded side and walks beneath the French balconies, from which old men in white singlets lean over the black fretwork, pruning with scissors, dropping cigarette ash onto the flagstones below. After forty minutes of dragging her heels, she decides to cross the tramlines and stroll beneath the trees of Shevchenko Park.

It is there that she happens to look up and see a man catch a sparrow in his hand. One moment the sparrow is flying with its head down, in search of crumbs; the next, the man's hand snatches it from the air. As quick as that. It bobs above his fingertips and all the young women come running to see and stroke the sparrow's head. But, once they surround the man, they realise he is not holding a sparrow but the head of his penis.

'No,' said Neil. 'No. Christ.'

'Exactly. See, it was a clever illusion.'

Now, for the benefit of those watching at a distance the man makes to release the sparrow. He opens his hand to the air, fluttering his fingertips, then walks off with one of the admiring women.

Neil was still stuck on the idea of the man whipping his cock out in Shevchencko Park, with women running towards him clutching their bags of bird feed.

The point I was trying to make is this: there were any number of strategies by which Neil might enter Judith's Russian neighbourhood, including sleight of hand, illusion. Now I came to my recommendation. Neil would have to impose himself on the landscape available and take possession of it.

Listen to what happens next in Shevchenko Park. Masha removes her shoes from her blistered heels. She happens to be sitting near a number of young men lined up at a kvass truck, clutching jars and pails. In another direction, through the trees at the edge of a small lake, she can make out a number of photographers in leather jackets circling a bride and groom. Eventually they depart for a distant caravan selling beer and vodka.

The couple soon follows. Masha says they couldn't bear to walk for more than a dozen paces without the bride coming to a halt and turning to her new husband with the words 'Kiss me.'

So they kiss and part, kiss and part, like butterflies. Masha watches them all the way back to the caravan where they melt into the crowd.

Only then does she discover an artist has set up his easel next to her. The man must have slipped in and made his preparations while she was absorbed by the bride and groom. The artist glances up, smiles and returns to his canvas.

The painting is of the bride and groom standing by the lake—the same view obtained through the trees, only brought into closer focus. Masha stares at the painting until, she said, she can feel the spirit of it enter into her, and when she gazes back in the direction of the wedding guests, it is her own face she sees on the bride. Through the trees in the distance she sees herself laughing, tossing her head back. It is her own face— the same one as in the painting—and she feels the same powerful longing that the young bride felt.

She snaps out of it only after an elderly man, a

veteran of the Great Patriotic War, chances by. He gives a polite cough and Masha opens her eyes to a jacket emblazoned with war medals. The Patriot politely averts his gaze as she makes the startling discovery that his hand is shoved up inside her blouse, cupping her breast. She withdraws that hand and the other plunges up her skirt.

She quite rightly kicked up a fuss. The Patriot shrugged and wandered off.

five

Neil proved to be an excellent student—almost too good, because Masha Venyukova's Odessa experience had immediate effect.

By now, the Owens were sleeping apart. Neil had set himself up in the spare room next door to the master bedroom. Two nights after I told him the tales from Shevchenko Park, he woke up on his camp stretcher wondering what had interrupted his sleep, then as he lay there the feeling grew in him that Mikhail was in bed with his wife in the next room. Sure enough, when he knelt with his ear to the wall, he heard noises that spoke of his wife's pleasure. The rustle of sheets, the careful shift of limbs, the long sighs.

So he crept out to the hall to stand in the doorway of Judith's room. There he remained like an interested spectator, watching his wife's hips rise beneath the duvet. He studied her smiling eyelids and the way her lips parted, and kissed, along a thin line of moisture. And then, he said, he noticed something quite different, something new in the way Judith twisted along the keel of her spine, that bit between her teeth—the unexpected vigour of it. Mikhail, he realised. Judith had brought him back to Neil's patch.

He left the hall, went out to the verandah and slipped around the side of the house to the bedroom window. There, he looked in and thought he saw Judith and the doctor lying across the bed. That's when the dance of the bride and groom in Shevchenko Park came back to him.

For the first time, he truly appreciated Masha's cleverness—to switch places with the bride. And how brilliant it would be now, were the doctor's lovesick penis to turn into a sparrow. No sooner did the thought occur than there was a feathery movement from Judith's loins, a flapping of wings. Both lovers stopped what they were doing and looked up, surprised, and the doctor knelt, said Neil, with his soft appendage folded in his hand.

*

Soon after this, Neil wanted to go to Russia. Nothing was going to stop him. I pictured Neil with his sleeves rolled up, marching through Mikhail's neighbourhood, looking out for the doctor's house. And I saw nothing but trouble ahead.

One afternoon we met at Wellington Railway Station for a practice run into Russia. I told Neil we had no choice but to make full use of the landscape available to us. Alert and interested as ever, he glanced about the station platforms for Russians. Point number three: the imagination is only a tool. We drive it with our will to rearrange the world to our liking. While still on the platform, I reminded Neil of the artist in Shevchenko Park and how he had borrowed Masha's features for the bride's. This too would be our *modus operandi*. First, though, I explained the need for his imagination to make room for the dimensions of Russia.

I told him to expect railway stations with a superior bearing. In Judith's Russia the stations are temples, the ceilings are pitched to the height of the gods. The roofs of the major railway stations are so high that at night the stars and moon shelter under them.

We sat in a carriage that was only a quarter full. In Russia, I said, the trains heave and breathe with humanity. While our trains are like someone hurrying through a crowd to get home, their trains convey a sense of epic; they move with a hip-rolling motion, a slow gathering of speed.

For the next forty minutes, all the way to Upper Hutt, I applied a Russian paintbrush to everything passing in the carriage window. As we came into stations I singled out a Russian face, though, as you might expect, few stand comparison. In Russia, Neil could expect faces to be more raw, like meat that has suffered freezer-burn. And he could expect old carbuncular women selling plain ice-cream from portable freezers. He liked me talking like that—'In Russia you can expect . . .' It gave him hope, prospects. I was getting into the swing of things. I pointed back at a Russian in beltless trousers looking forlornly up from the fallen-down trellis in his backyard.

As the train flew by a section of state housing, Neil closed his eyes at my command, and I talked him through a Moldavian neighbourhood of small circular cottages made of splintered timber, plaster walls painted an indigo colour to ward off evil, and tea-cosy roofs of thatched bulrushes.

Near Naenae, where the walls of the valley close, the hills covered in the yellow flower of gorse and broom filled the top part of the carriage window. Take away the broom and the gorse and these same hills could be found fringing Judith's Russian neighbourhood—although with another slight difference. If we may refer to a hill as a man, then in the Ukraine the man is shorter and cleaner shaven.

I told Neil to think of Moldavia as a gentle short man in round glasses. Many of them. Row upon row of gentlemen in glasses, humble clerks rising from desks, one after another, from the east of the Ukraine all the way to the Romanian border.

The lessons had been going several months now. Twice a week, Neil drove over the hill to my flat in Wellington. I don't know where he told his wife he was going. And as summer shifted from this part of the world, his impatience found new expression.

One afternoon he showed up at my door looking shamefaced. Some unpleasantness had gone down at home the previous night. He had started drinking early in the evening and later stood on his camp stretcher shouting in Russian through the bedroom wall.

Of course, by now he was desperate to break into Judith's Russia, to make his smash-and-grab and dust her off from her Russian adventure. I cautioned that certain experiences lay outside his grasp. Winter, for example. He had no idea how brutal it could be. I suppose I was nervous of failing him as well. I cribbed stories from the library—accounts of Siberian cities where frozen crows announce the arrival of spring by toppling from window ledges, and small children run to gather up the black ornamental pieces to thread into necklaces and wear as good-luck charms to ward off pneumonia. Or the fate of drunks in old Tsarist Russia, of fellows with a skinful driving sleighs into snow-drifts, and dawn finding their expressions of hilarity gnawed down to the bone by the wild dogs of Moscow.

The stories were meant to be cautionary. But at the same time they allowed Neil to see how Russia could attract and detain his wife after the temperate character of the Wairarapa.

There was one thing I had almost overlooked. I hadn't invented a character for Neil. He couldn't possibly venture into Russia looking the way he did. Judith's Russia was Old Russia with its horses and carts and peasants squatting in the fields. We couldn't have him bounding in there with a pair of Nikes. I told him he would need another identity. I knew just the place to find one. We bundled into Neil's ute and I directed him to the night shelter. We parked opposite and studied the shuffling lines, the bearded barefoot men in coats; others with running sores, mumbling curses into their matted beards. They would have been holy men

in Tsarist Russia. *Yurodivy* describes the pious traveller, barefoot, ragged, bringing news and stories from
far away.

My idea was for Neil to enter Judith's world by this
subterfuge; dressed in rags, he would ghost from one
world through to the other.

six

The cheques kept rolling in, and throughout the
summer Neil absorbed my stories and my local Russian
landscapes. I'm going to pinch one of Neil's words here
to describe a 'mulching' process. Most market garden-
ers these days use black polyethylene—Neil says there
is no better ground-cover protection. But for feeding
and nourishment you can't really go past a mulch of
wet straw and leaves. What is laid around the plant
eventually ends up inside the plant. That's the miracle
of mulch.

Point number four: time is the other element at play.
Time will stare down the pyramids, eventually.

If I explain how Neil was able to enter Judith's
kingdom then it is important to keep hold of the idea
of mulch—or the ground I prepared with Masha
Venyukova's stories, her experiences with the Turk,

the sparrow and the artist of Shevchenko Park and, of course, my own descriptions from the carriage window.

It was late March when Neil dreamt his way into Judith's Russia. Why this night and not another? Why does a plant choose that particular moment to burst through the last layer of soil into daylight?

When he later reported back he described the wet rooftops of Odessa, the grey rectangular areas between the buildings that divide the Black Sea.

Neil is comforted to find everything in its place, and familiar. Over there, that must be the Odessa Railway Station. A line of crows sits along the top of the copper-roofed pergola. Outside the station is a flea market where women stand elbow to elbow, making clothes-hangers out of their limbs to display blouses for sale, and men sell dill out of black leather caps. The only thing that is challengingly new is a sweet smell of old sweat that he traces to the bedrolls on the top bunks. Otherwise he feels the same unhurried hip-rolling movement of the train. On the slow climb to Kishinev, he gazes out at the slightly rounded, clerical aspect of the hills.

He watches the countryside pass slowly. Bulrushes, this paddock, that paddock, bulrushes again. Another hill, another bald clerk rising from his desk, then another.

He left in daylight, but it is dark when he reaches Kishinev. And it is not until he leaves the train and steps onto the platform that he feels the cold sensation of the unfamiliar. He looks down to discover he is barefoot. And there, in the window, is the reflection of a stranger—the ragged reflection of a Russian tramp. A tangled beard, a rat's nest of hair. As Neil raises his hand the figure in the window does the same; the same hand appears to touch the same beard, nose and chin.

I had told Neil to look out for a priest's grave to sleep beside—to ensure he would go unmolested by roaming mobs. Look for the graves planted with blue forget-me-nots. But in what direction? Where, for god's sake? The tremors of panic are stirring in his belly. The air is astonishingly cold and his thoughts are full of the stories I have told him—of Russia's past invaders turning to ice mid-stride; of Napoleon's men lying awake at night, afraid their breath will freeze over and block their breathing passages. He remembers that in the depths of winter a spoken word can quickly turn to ice inside one's mouth. In this way a skull may creak open with the name of a loved one. This is why in Russian post-cards we see so many corpses with their mouths stretched wide. Some even with their mouths bandaged, to ensure the name of their loved one will escort them to their grave. On the platform in Kishinev, Neil is thinking of those skulls wrenched slowly open with the longer names of Henrietta, Rebecca, Josephine, when a man with a lantern pushes forward out of the shadows.

'Friend, have you come far?' The man measures Neil up close, then lowers the light to crouch beside his running sores. He shakes his head and advises Neil to have the wounds seen to. 'Without proper treatment they will soon fester.' He rises, spits on the ground and looks around. 'The doctor's house is not far from here. I'll take you there, myself.'

So this is Russia. So this is the night. Russian air. Neil is alert to every possible detail. Along the way the kind stranger offers him words of encouragement. Soon the nights will be warm and the countryside will recover its senses.

After a short while, the horse's rear hoof comes to rest and the driver leans forward to point with his whip to a lit window set back from the road. 'There is the doctor,' he says.

Neil thanks the driver. He struggles down and lands gingerly. He can't believe his luck so far.

The driver's parting words are 'Pray for me.'

In the doctor's garden a great variety of scents cling to the air, among them the green scent of unripe tomatoes. But it is too dark to see. In the distance Neil can hear the soft slapping progress of the horse. He takes another step towards the window and a chicken splashes out from under his feet.

He counts to twenty and sets off again for the window.

There is Judith, sitting by the fire grate with a lace frame on her lap. Naturally Neil is beside himself with excitement. He is thrilled, full of achievement and wonder. All caution is tossed aside as he moves more fully in to the window.

She seems content. Or is that little frown for the needlework or for some general condition? He is mulling this over when Judith looks up and sees him in the window. He cups his hands, as if he's about to explain. He wants to reassure her. But she is pointing at him, her hand raised. Her eyes, mouth, everything is pegged to the outer limits of alarm.

'It's me, Neil,' he says back at the window.

But no—she apparently doesn't recognise him. It's clear that when she's in Russia he doesn't exist, which is what he suspected all along. He is still digesting this unpleasant fact when there is a rush of air—a heavy hand falls upon him and Mikhail's Russian breath fills his ear. There are dark threats, bold plans of punishment as he is dragged round to the courtyard.

But in the light everything changes.

'Why, my poor fellow. Look at you.' The doctor pokes around the infected areas of his shins. 'Did some kind soul send you here?'

Then Judith calls out from inside the cottage, 'Who is it, Mikhail? Did you catch him?'

They could be back in the Wairarapa. It could be Judith calling back from the garden to ask who telephoned.

'Just a poor traveller in need of running repair,' answers Mikhail.

Mikhail is less imposing than Neil had thought. Beetle-browed. A small, puckered mouth—not like his own, which is long and thin-lipped. He wonders if Judith has difficulty adjusting. She likes to kiss.

'Inside with you, good sir,' says the doctor. 'I need to clean those wounds.'

Inside is wonderfully warm, but Neil hardly dares to raise his eyes in case Judith recognises him beneath his tramp's garb.

'Wait by the grate. There's a good fellow,' says Mikhail.

Judith is on the far side of the room, but even from that distance Neil said he could feel her hostility. Now she unleashes it on Mikhail. Why must the tramp violate their privacy? Why must he stay the night? Hadn't the doctor done enough already? The doctor smiles good-naturedly. He is amused by the spirit shown by his pet golubchik. He reminds her that it is good luck to provide a pious wanderer with shelter. They should be so lucky that their house was chosen. More so to have the tramp arrive at the end of winter. This way, luck will shine upon them for only a brief period of inconvenience.

'He can sleep by the grate,' continues the doctor. 'And when he gets better, I will set him to work in the garden. In another two weeks it will be spring. There will be cherry blossom in the trees, fresh grass for his bed. He can get on his way then.'

In the morning, Neil woke in a ball at the end of his camp stretcher. He was still in Russia, shivering by the grey embers. A small bird must have flown against the window because he looked up and saw the Belgian elms outside and, in the distance, a pohutukawa. He remembered that Judith had wanted to turn him out.

For the rest of the day he was short with her, yelling at her at the slightest opportunity—for standing the cutlery up the wrong way in the dishwasher, for leaving the butter out, for leaving the oven elements on.

But this is not the way Mikhail treats his little bird in Russia. They never argue. It's remarkable, said Neil.

Well, there was that disagreement over his arrival. Otherwise Judith has only to ask for something for it to be hers. There is just the one thing denied her, and that is her memory of another life. The moment the events of the rape and violence bubble from her, Mikhail is quick to act. He seals her lips with a little nonsense. He babies her, shush-shushes her, rubs the darkness from her neck, her shoulders, her loins.

At night, said Neil, the doctor sits in his rocker and runs his eyes over his beautiful captive—closing in on the fault. Something is not quite right with her jawbone; something is weighing it down at the rear, and it makes her eyes pool with apprehension. She appears to be constantly on the verge of fright. This does not reflect well on him, of course, so he rocks in his chair, scratching his chin. He ponders and dreams up ways to correct this defect. If only the darkness would shift from the back of her eyes, then she might take her place with the other young, confident women of Russian parentage, and stroll about with a parasol in Pushkin Park.

Neil sees more clearly at night—the doctor's motives, his wife's captivity, everything that Judith cannot see for herself. On the other hand, he might as well be wallpaper, for Judith barely acknowledges him. She relays any request or comment through Raisa, the doctor's trusted servant.

Still, at night he has the freedom of the house. In the dead hours he may stand in the bedroom doorway and watch the love-making of Judith and Mikhail. The doctor is always in his nightshirt and nightcap, all rigging and sail; and Judith is all arms and legs, trying to haul in the mainsheet.

Neil had an idea that if he could return to Russia with a shred of evidence from Judith's old life, that might be enough to jolt her away from Mikhail's grasp.

But he needed to act soon. In Mikhail's garden everything speaks of quick awakening. Green buds have burst along grey limbs. During the day the air is lazy and warm. Soon the doctor will have no reason to detain him and Neil will pass from the doctor's charity out of Judith's life for good.

seven

Another day and he finds a small section of Mikhail's garden wall collapsed. He steps through and feels the abrupt shift from solidity and guardedness to the shrieks and cries of young children chasing each other up the strada. He moves along to an intact section and places his eye to a hairline crack in the wall. His plan requires that he be furtive. Judith arrives, trailing breadcrumbs beneath the bedsheets hanging in the trees near the primrose. She is sweet-talking the chickens. Zdes' Anna. Tam Marya. Privet, Aleksandr. As she ventures out to the garden she inhales new scents; once she draws such a deep breath of satisfaction that Neil experiences a change of heart. She appears happy, does she not? Content with Mikhail in his garden. Perhaps he should respect that and withdraw. The feeling soon passes.

By good fortune, it appears that Judith will end up at the garden seat by the wall. She is in no hurry though. There are so many peonies to admire and welcome into existence. A name to be invented for each one. She pats the head of a tulip. And as she reaches the last of her 'children', Neil calls to her the names of old schoolmates and TV programs from her childhood in the Pacific. As each of these old acorns lands, she looks up, interested the second and third time.

'Sandy?' she says, lightly. She is staring back at the wall, directly at the crack behind which Neil crouches with a big grin, and she raises a white glove to her chest. 'Is that really you? Havelock Girls?' Her eyes light up with a happy thought. 'Are you still holding your breath underwater?' Then she has another idea. 'Hello, I'm Mister Ed. Chomp. Chomp.'

Neil is smiling happily. This is progress. It is short-lived, however. There is a silvery movement of a trout moving out from the shadows. Over Judith's shoulder, he sees Raisa, her arms filled with washing. Her head is turned to listen to Judith chatting away at the wall. She dumps the washing and bends down for a clod of earth.

As the dirt explodes against the wall, there is a gasp from Judith, and Neil delays a moment with all the things left unsaid. 'Judith . . .' is all he has time for.

When he thought about it later he was slightly disappointed by its plaintiveness—too much like the last words of a drowning person, he felt—and he disappears up the strada with the foul-mouthed Raisa in pursuit.

In the Wairarapa, Neil behaved like a jilted lover. He had nothing to say to Judith at the breakfast table. They made for different parts of the garden. He retired from Judith's peacemaking efforts. Neil had made up his mind that the affair could only be sorted out in Russia.

The next night he slopes back to Mikhail's. He picks his way through the garden. This time no chicken rushes from under his feet as he approaches the window.

Judith is in her favourite chair by the fire grate,

reading. Mikhail enters the room and Judith looks up from her book. She smiles as if all the secrets in the world are known to her, and it strikes Neil, standing at the window, how much she has grown in confidence. Mikhail drops onto a knee to pay homage to her thigh. If she has gained and prospered from her time in Russia, then equally, it seems to Neil, Mikhail has conceded something. She is now the column and the doctor is the ivy.

The names and TV programs Neil lobbed over the garden wall have lasted no longer than a child's patience with a new toy. This is hardly what he had hoped for, or for that matter what I so confidently predicted— that the words from Judith's other world would act as trapeze rings for her to grasp hold of so she could swing out and over the wall, away from Russia and this captivity.

Neil is still moping at the window when from the street comes the sound of running footsteps. The gate latch is fumbled; there is a quick dash across the flag-stones in the courtyard. At the sound of someone banging at the door, Mikhail looks up from Judith's thigh and reluctantly drags himself away.

Some of the conversation is clear to Neil, only because the woman is repeating herself out of panic. There has been an accident. Her husband failed to rise after falling from a milking stool. He was sitting . . . where she left him . . . on the milking stool. Then when she returned he was unconscious. 'Please, he will not wake.'

Neil retreats to the shadows until he hears the doctor's carriage rattle away down the street. Then he returns to the window and there, inside the cottage, Judith is alone—for the first time.

The thought must have occurred to her as well, because she smiles. They both do. Then Judith settles back in her chair. She picks up her book and finds her place. Almost immediately she looks up again. It is as if she is at home, in the Wairarapa, when she has left it too late to read and her eyes skate over the text. She rises to her feet and in a single motion raises her dress over her shoulders and drops it to the floor. Next she removes her bra. Her breasts topple out and she folds her arms beneath them and shifts closer to the grate. She has returned to the matter which perplexed her earlier. She looks down and thinks to step out of her underwear. Neil watches the spring in her pubic hair unfold. A dull expression enters his wife's face, as if she is unsure of what to do next. She gazes about the room, scratches her crotch, and departs for bed.

*

At least an hour has passed. There has been no sign of Mikhail. It seems a long time since the lamps in the bedroom went out, and all this time Neil has stood shivering in his bare feet. Now he makes his move.

As he expected, the door off the courtyard has been left open, and Neil creeps through the house to the bedroom. He has decided he will wake Judith and explain everything in full. She needs to hear an impartial voice in order to understand properly what has happened to her—the doctor's sly manipulation of her memory and his scheming from the outset when he scraped her off the road and brought her home to be his mistress.

But in the bedroom Neil has second thoughts. If he wakes her, is there any guarantee that she will see the right person? What if she only recognises the bedraggled tramp whom she scorns and detests? There is another way. He would never have thought of it but for Mikhail's nightgown and nightcap slung over the back of a chair.

Quietly he changes his rags for the doctor's bedclothes. The nightshirt is tight around the shoulders and there is a loud tear when Neil reaches up to place the doctor's nightcap on his head. Judith stirs, and Neil holds his position—an arm raised above his head—

until her breathing resumes its normal pattern. Then he moves to the doctor's side of the bed.

The bed feels strangely unaccommodating and an anecdote from another invasion comes to Neil's mind. He recalls the surprise of the French at finding Moscow abandoned—this is something I had described to him—their tiptoeing about the Kremlin apartments, watched by a caged bird, the clocks tick-tocking, while they tried on Russian shoes and stretched out on their beds, tossing fitfully to make a narrow ravine in a mattress where there already existed a valley. Neil finds he has the opposite problem. The doctor has left only a shallow and narrow impression upon the mattress.

Later, Neil wondered what it was that woke Judith. What was she responding to? Was it this primal act of invasiveness—or was it a feeling of difference?

There is none of the desperate eagerness which he had witnessed between Judith and Mikhail. Rather, she stirs contentedly, like a sunbather. From the depths of sleep a smile rises on her face, and her hand reaches for the doctor's nightshirt. She must have smelt Mikhail on him. Neil finds himself smiling at how easy it is. So easy. Criminally easy. Nothing more enters into it, not guilt, or doubt, just this—as Judith receives him, that everything is so wonderfully familiar, it is back to old times.

eight

A drunk staggers up the wrong path, into the wrong house, through the wrong door and into the wrong bed. And what happens? The woman drowsily commences making love to the man she assumes is her partner.

Lawyers say it's not nearly as uncommon as you might think. The legal questions tend to probe the area of awareness, 'the quality of the act', and, of course, the response of the perpetrator once the alarm is raised. Did he go on breathlessly to the end, doggedly pursuing his satisfaction? Or did he sit up, confused, embarrassed, apologetic, at a loss for words, then quickly dress and lace up his shoes?

Neil watches his wife's thoughts come and go in order—surprise, betrayal, disgust. She closes her eyes, thinking perhaps it is another dream, but when she opens them again, Neil is still there.

She sits up in bed and snatches at the bedding, dragging it around herself. Then she snaps at him to hand her the pillow. The moment seems to be full of embarrassing transitions until Judith's disgust takes full hold. She demands to know what he is smiling at—just what the hell is there to smile at?

'Raisa . . .' he starts to say. Something to do with

Judith's gathering the bedding around her reminds him of Raisa bundling the washing in her arms. 'The primrose?' he says, hoping everything can be referred back to Mikhail's neighbourhood. He repeats what she had said to Raisa: 'Spread the sheets over the primrose.'

But none of it makes any sense. Judith doesn't appear to remember. She looks at him without comprehension. She shakes her head and falls back in bed, still with the bedding wrapped around her. She tells him she's heard all she wants to for now. He can switch off the light on his way out. Whatever he has to say for himself can wait until morning.

Neil lies awake the rest of the night pondering the whole messy business. He would have said whatever it took to make things right again, but when he thinks of what the explanation amounts to—the past months spent on Russian drills, my involvement, Masha Venyukova, my next-door neighbour, this fleshing-out of an imaginary landscape in order to pursue his wife—the invasion gathers more heft, and so, come morning, he finds he has nothing to say.

Neil turned up at my door later that afternoon, an air of bereavement about him.

'Judith's gone,' he said. She'd packed a bag and caught a bus to Napier. She planned to stay with her parents until Neil 'got himself together'. 'I can't believe she's gone.'

'Only temporarily,' I boldly assured him. 'She'll be back.'

But he answered this with a gloomy look. 'She took the wedding photographs.'

She must have experienced a change of heart. Maybe she spoke to someone with a nose for the legal angle in this mess, because a week later a policeman arrived at Neil's door. This is how I came to public notice, as a witness in Mrs Owen's charge of rape against her husband.

Neil turned up to a preliminary hearing in a shiny suit. He engaged a lawyer who was prepared to argue that Neil thought he was in Russia at the time. This is when the newspapers became interested and the whole thing ended up at my door.

I became something of a celebrity. 'Dream-Maker'. That's how my name got about. There were television appearances, radio interviews. I got wild calls in the middle of the night, slurred voices that spoke of errant partners running off with waiters and rodeo riders to distant corners of the globe. Argentina to Tennessee. And what could I do to lead them into the dreamscape of their smitten husbands and wives?

Judith looked around at the circus she had created and decided she had had enough. She dropped the charges. On the morning of our last day in court, we bumped into each other and she asked if we could have a private chat. One of the interview rooms wasn't being used, so we went in there. I suppose she was Neil's age—thirty-eight, -nine, thereabouts. She had the same manner as Neil, which I mistook for shyness. She glanced downwards, but then when she spoke, like Neil, she was direct and to the point.

She said, 'My counsel will be here in a few minutes, so I'll do the talking, shall I?' She smiled, half in apology I suspect, because she began by saying that Neil was one of the most unimaginative men she had ever met. 'You must be a very clever man.'

'Well, Neil was a good student,' I said.

She didn't respond to that. She said, 'You probably want to know why Russia, Mikhail. I'm not even sure I know the full answer. But I do know this. When you work the land, you learn to study it very carefully. You know every clod of dirt, every new shoot. And you know everything there is to know about one another—Neil and me. Neil's tired love-making. I don't know if I should mention that.'

I coughed and looked away.

'No. Probably I shouldn't.' She fumbled in her bag

for a cigarette. I lit a match for her, and she continued. 'Mikhail isn't anything to write home about, but it's enough that he's different. Attentive, wildly possessive, oh, heavens, yes.' She thrilled to that, wriggling in her white coat. She laughed. 'All those roses and gifts, bathing me, dancing at night in the garden. You think you'll never fall for it . . .

'Anyway. Russia.' She blew a smoke ring up to the ceiling. 'Russia was my room at the end of the hall. I don't know if you're familiar with that expression. It's something my father used to say to us girls: "Your mother's in the room at the end of the hall"—which was code for saying she was out of bounds. That room was like another country which she kept secret from us kids.

'Once I asked to see inside it, and she said, "There's nothing to see." She opened the door to a bare room. She put a finger to her lips, then she said, "Can you hear it?"

"Hear what?" I asked. Well, I couldn't hear anything.

"Hear the waterfall," she said. "Close your eyes. Listen. Now can you hear?"

"Yes," I said—even though I couldn't. But I was ten and I thought I was supposed to hear the waterfall like I was supposed to know how to spell universe and that

Peking was the capital of China. I didn't want to disappoint her.

'Now of course I know what she was talking about. I understand now. If there was a waterfall, then you can bet there was a pond. I think of my mother in one of her summer dresses, picnicking with one of the farmers from the tennis club.'

There were voices in the hall outside.

Judith looked up and continued. 'I didn't believe Neil when he told me about finding his way to Mikhail's.'

'And now?'

'And now . . . I don't know, except for this. I'll ask you to keep your imagination to yourself in the future. It can be a dangerous thing when you spread it around.'

nine

Two years have flown by since the Owens were together in Russia. They have shared memories; they have private memories. They have agreed that what went on in Mikhail's bedroom should stay behind a closed door.

As you might expect, their memories are starting to fragment. Sometimes Judith will see a flower or inhale a scent that in a blink takes her right back to Mikhail's garden. She remembers the lime-washed walls and the way the trees enclosed the cottage. She often finds herself thinking about the stillness of stone walls—like the eyes of dead cows piled one upon the other. Or Neil will see something on TV—a BBC travelogue down the Volga—and a dirt road recalls the strada he ran down with Raisa in pursuit, or—and this happened recently—he rang to say a funny little fellow from Inland Revenue had turned up to audit their GST returns, and Neil said he couldn't stop smiling at the man's round glasses and shining forehead, thinking of Moldavia.

The Old Country, as they've come to call it. 'My little bird . . . My golubchik . . .' The Owens joke among themselves. 'And one for my pet golubchik,' Neil will say when pouring a glass of wine for Judith.

But there are other times, like at fundraising dances for the local play centre (the Owens have a pair of daughters now), after dancing with the mad, grinning plumber and tolerating the bank clerk pushing his groin into her, that Judith misses Mikhail, and recalls a night in Kishinev when he expertly made use of the entire garden and they danced on air for hours. Or on those days when rain has completely obscured the view out the window and there is nothing to do but stand before it with folded arms, her thoughts wander back to Russia. She remembers when Mikhail bathed her and how he renamed her landscape.

She also remembers what it is to fall out of love and into love, and how, sometimes, the two things can happen concurrently, like departure and arrival, or the shifting status of two countries called 'home'.

Read more ...

Lloyd Jones

HAND ME DOWN WORLD

Sometimes a person passes through your world and you don't forget them

She is like that.

She is crossing continents, searching for her missing child.

Everyone she comes into contact with has a tale to tell: the truck driver who mistook her for a prostitute, the hunters who almost shot her, the Frenchman who loved her, the blind man and the lodger.

This is her story.

'A moving and inspiring read . . . A truly spellbinding story that will leave you reflecting on it for days' *Stylist*

'One of the most significant novelists writing today' *Sunday Times*

'Jones's novel is haunting to the very final line' *Sunday Telegraph*

'Everyone will want to read *Hand Me Down World* and few will be able to stop thinking about it after they do' *Irish Independent*

Order your copy now by calling Bookpoint on 01235 827716 or visit your local bookshop quoting ISBN 978-1-84854-480-2 www.johnmurray.co.uk

Read more ...

Lloyd Jones

MISTER PIP

Shortlisted for the Man Booker Prize

Winner of the Commonwealth Writers' Prize

On a lush island in the South Pacific, civil war threatens daily life. Thirteen-year-old Matilda and her friends haven't seen the inside of a classroom for months until the village recluse emerges to breathe life back into an old book. Surrounded by the constant threat of violence, their new teacher introduces the children to a boy named Pip and a man called Mr Dickens. But on an island at war, the power of stories can have deadly consequences.

'Haunting and morally complex' *Sunday Times*

'A brilliantly nuanced examination of the power of imagination' *Financial Times*

'One of the best books of the year!' Isabel Allende

Order your copy now by calling Bookpoint on 01235 827716 or visit your local bookshop quoting ISBN 978-0-7195-6994-4 www.johnmurray.co.uk

Read more ...

Lloyd Jones

BIOGRAFI

A remarkable tale by the author of *Mister Pip*

Once a humble dentist, Peter Shapallo was plucked from his modest
family life and surgically enhanced to serve for thirty years as the
body double for the brutal Albanian dictator, Enver Hoxha. Or was
he?

Equal parts travelogue, political reportage and bizarre mystery novel,
Lloyd Jones's remarkable tale takes us across Albania as it reinvents
itself – a volatile, surreal wonderland where nothing is quite as it
seems and no one is who they appear to be.

'Beautifully written, evocative and deft' *Sunday Times*

'Extraordinarily haunting' *Daily Telegraph*

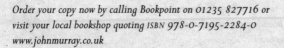

*Order your copy now by calling Bookpoint on 01235 827716 or
visit your local bookshop quoting ISBN 978-0-7195-2284-0
www.johnmurray.co.uk*

Read more . . .

Lloyd Jones

HERE AT THE END OF THE WORLD WE LEARN TO DANCE

Fall in love in the course of one dance

In a cave set back from the ocean, on the coast of New Zealand, Louise and Schmidt hide along with two local boys frightened of being called up to fight in the Great War. But the sensual rhythm of the tango lessons which Schmidt teaches on that sandy cave floor will have devastating consequences for all of them. Two generations later, Schmidt's fiery granddaughter Rosa captivates a young man with the same sultry music that inspired seduction and deception so many years before.

'It sounds so light-hearted – a story about dance and love – and yet it is also so ineffably sad, just like the tango itself, heartbreaking and exhilarating . . . A skilfully constructed book . . . very rich, but never hard work' *New Zealand Herald*

Order your copy now by calling Bookpoint on 01235 827716 or visit your local bookshop quoting ISBN 978-0-7195-2403-5
www.johnmurray.co.uk

Read more . . .

Lloyd Jones

THE BOOK OF FAME

In this melding of true history and imagination, Lloyd Jones has recreated an unforgettable journey from innocence to celebrity

In August 1905 a party of young men set sail for England. Amongst them were ordinary farmers and bootmakers, a miner and a bank clerk. Together they made up the All Blacks, an unknown rugby team from Auckland, New Zealand. Far from home, weary, bedazzled and a little lost, they had come to show the world what they could do.

What they didn't know was that they were bound for fame.

'Jones proves sly, engaging, worth reading and even re-reading'
London Review of Books

Order your copy now by calling Bookpoint on 01235 827716 or visit your local bookshop quoting ISBN 978-0-7195-2294-9
www.johnmurray.co.uk